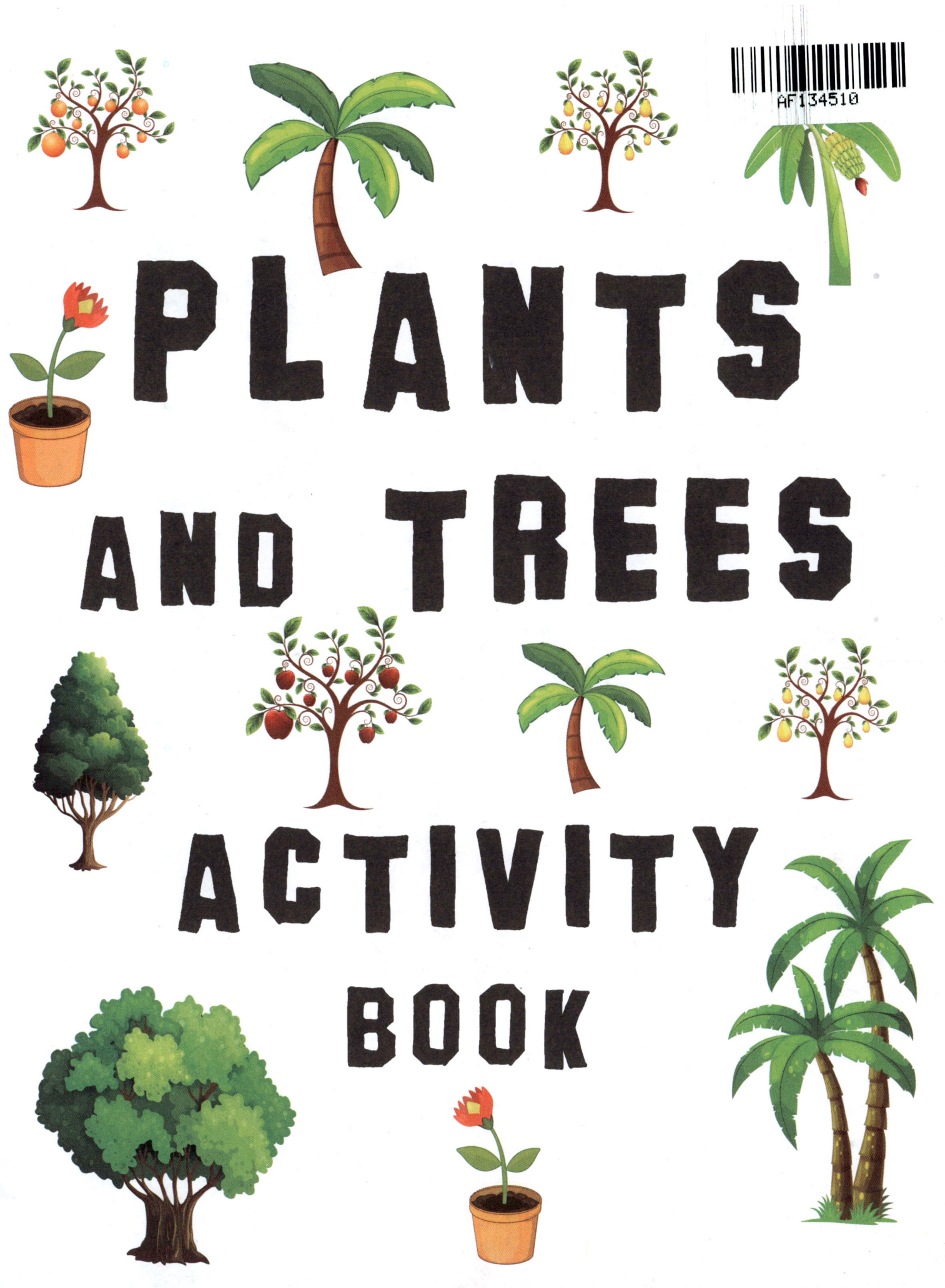

 Label the parts of the plant and the tree and understand the difference.

 Root is the portion below the ground. We eat roots of many plants. Circle the edible root plants.

 Draw a line from the name of the part of the plant to its picture.

Flower

Leaf

Roots

Stem

 Paste five leaves of different trees and name them.

5 Given below is the shoot system of a plant. Join the words with their corresponding picture.

Leaf

Flower

Fruit

Stem

6 Colour your thumb with different colours and press the coloured thumb on paper to create leaves. Repeat this practice until the tree is full of leaves.

 Identify the trees and draw a line matching the tree names with their pictures.

Fir tree

Banana tree

Coconut tree

Banyan Tree

8 Paste a leaf from the following trees.

Fir tree | Banyan tree | Royal Poinciana | Oak tree | Ash tree

9 Circle the things that are made from trees.

10 A conversation between a tree and a boy

Tree: Hey, little champ. Where are you going?

Boy: Hi F I R T R _ E. I'm going to school.

Tree: Hey, do you know me?

Boy: Yes, everybody does. Trees are important to humans. They provide us FRU_TS and VEGET_BLES to eat, OX_GEN to breathe, SH_DE in summer and protect us from CO_D winds in winter.

Tree: You know so much about me. I'm impressed.

Boy: I also know that you provide us WO_D to make FUR_ITURE and many other useful things.

Tree: That's right. I think you must go to school now and learn many more things.

Boy: Ok, Bye.

11

Trees grow from seeds. Given below is the lifecycle of an Oak tree. Colour the picture.

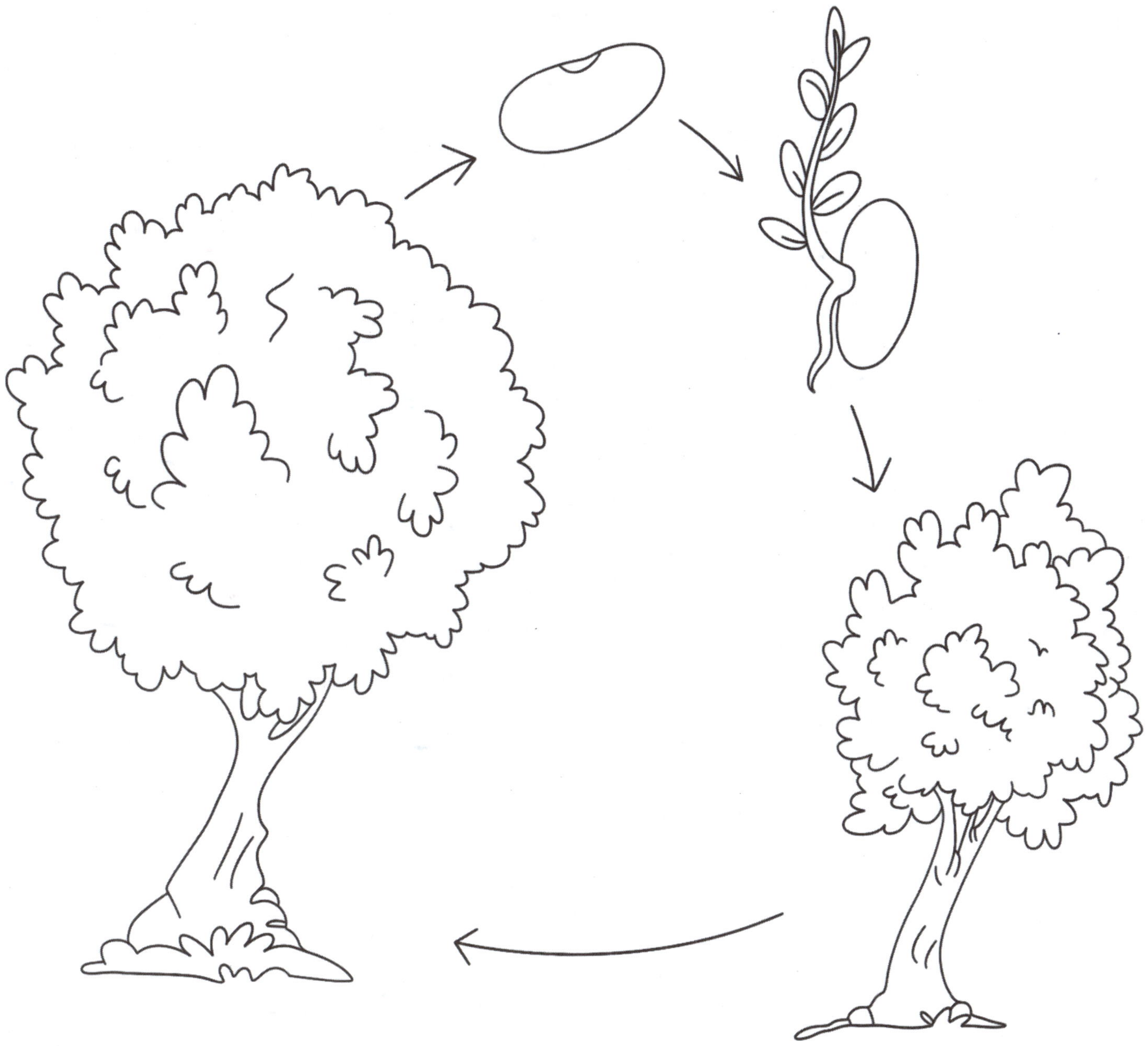

12 Colour the tree and label its parts.

 Match the correct options.

Trees give us

Trees grow from

Root vegetables

Shoot plant

14 Trees are important to us as they give us oxygen and take in carbon dioxide released by us. Draw suitable arrows to depict the same.

15 Join the dots to complete the picture and colour it.

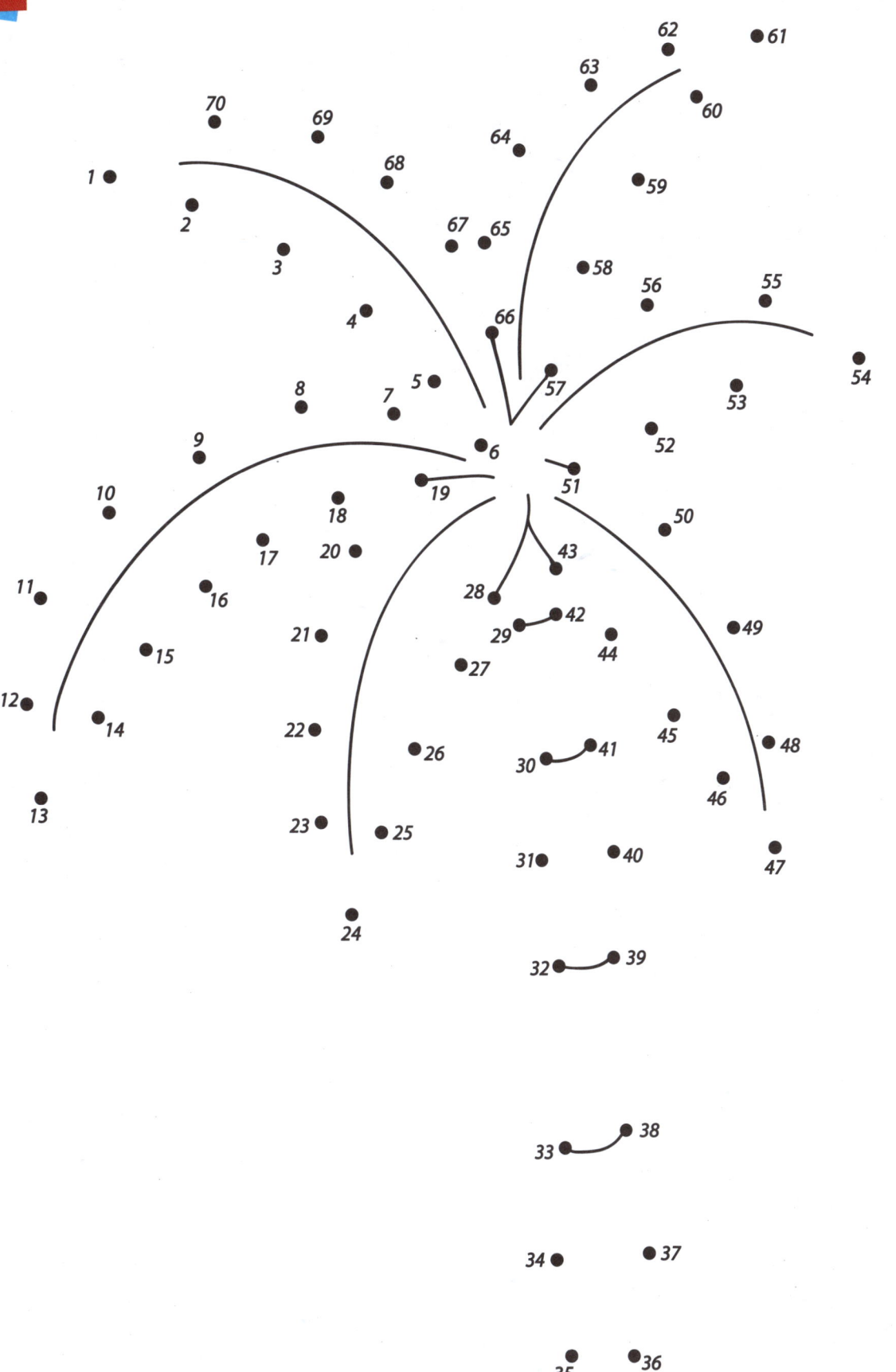

15

16 Connect the dots to complete the tree.

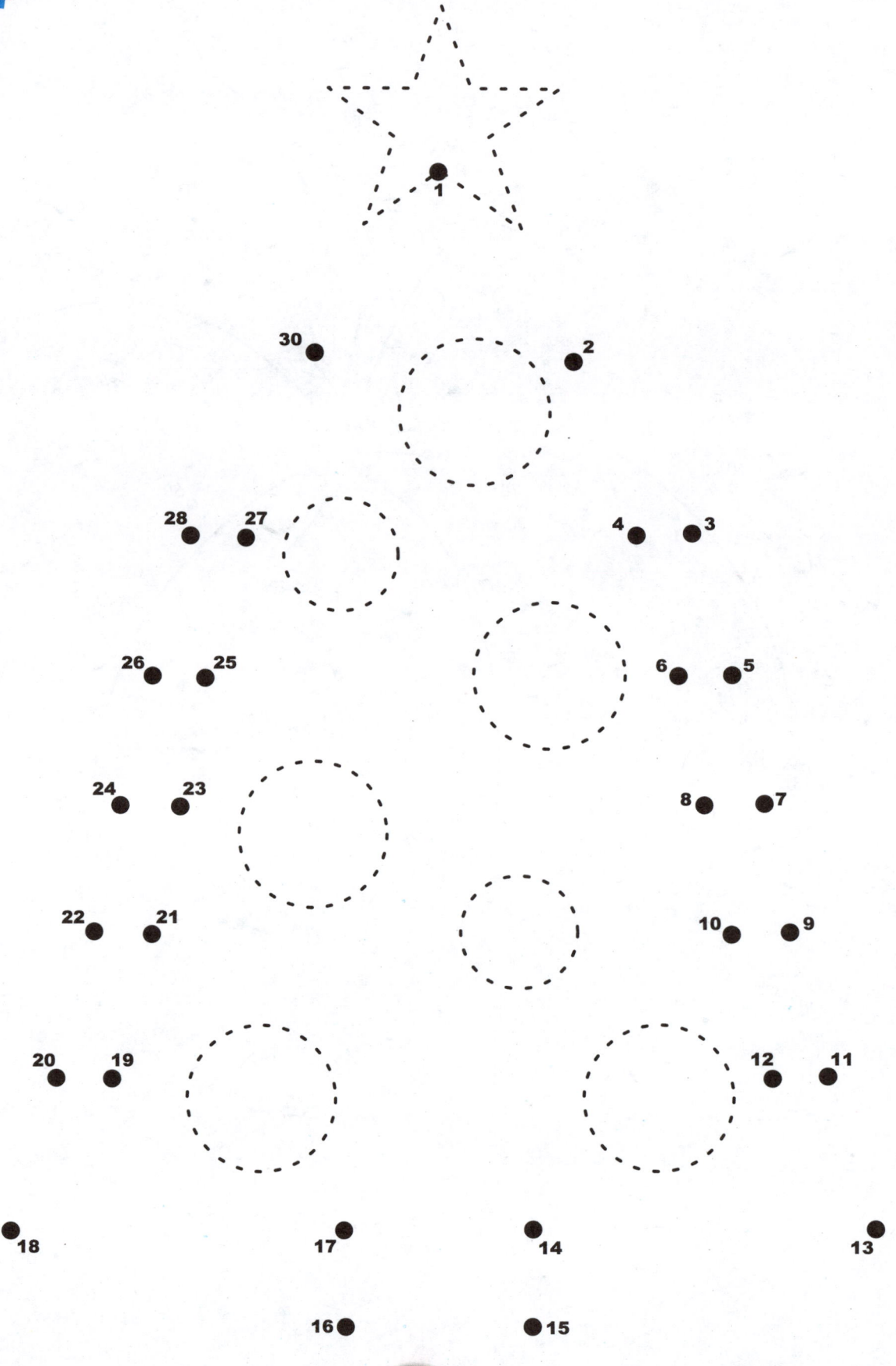

17 Pick out tall trees and circle them.

 **Distinguish between the leaves and match them with their names.**

Horse chestnut tree leaf

Ash tree leaf

Maple tree leaf

Elder tree leaf

Birch tree leaf

19 Pick out short trees and circle them.

20 Photosynthesis is a process by which plants make their food with the help of sunlight, water and carbon dioxide. Draw the missing elements in the picture.

21

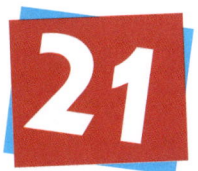

Put a tick beside conifer trees and cross against those which are not.

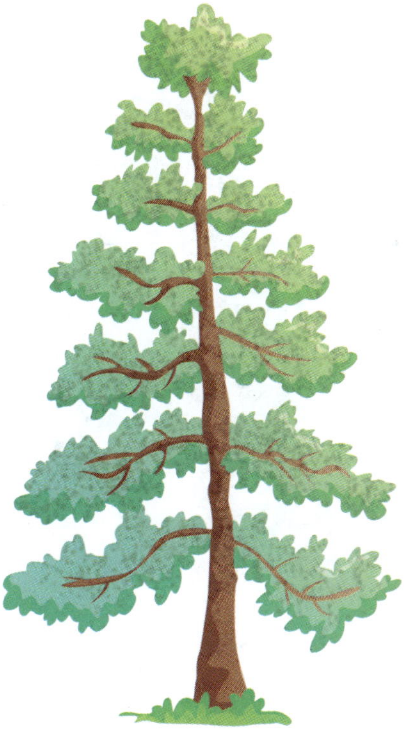
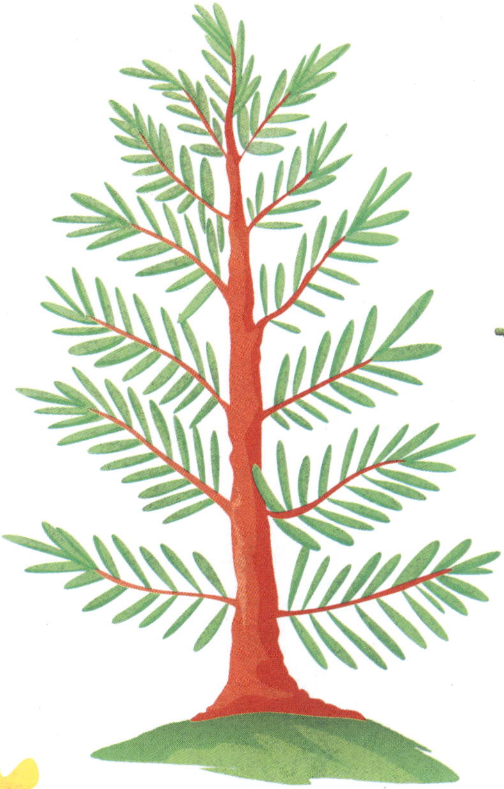
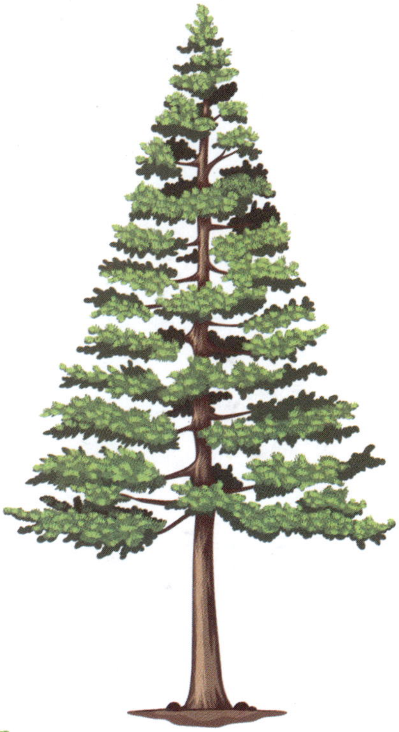
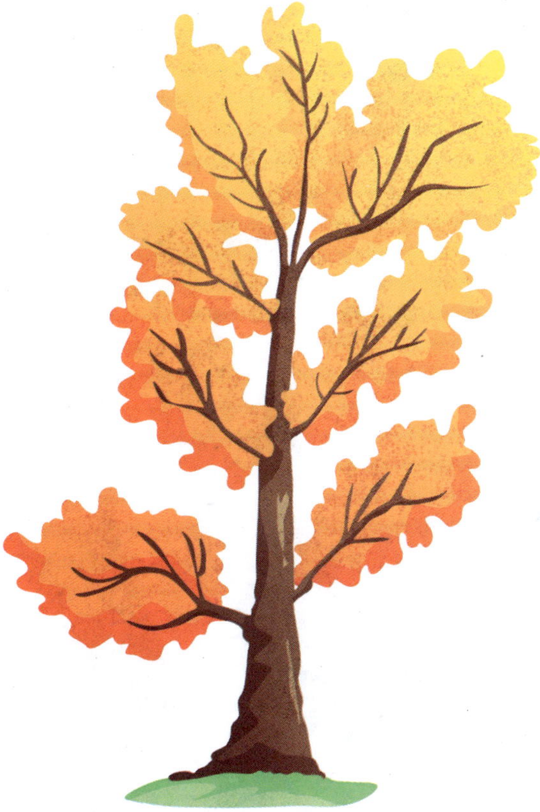
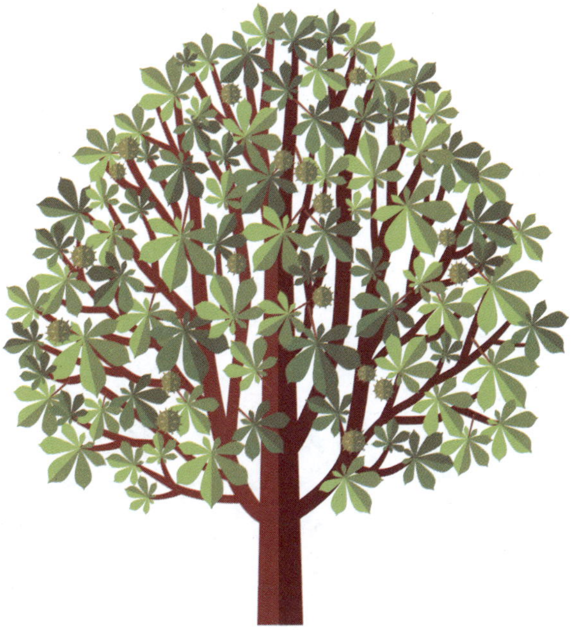

22 Circle the leaves with spines.

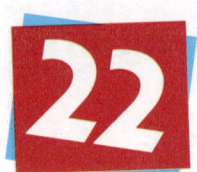

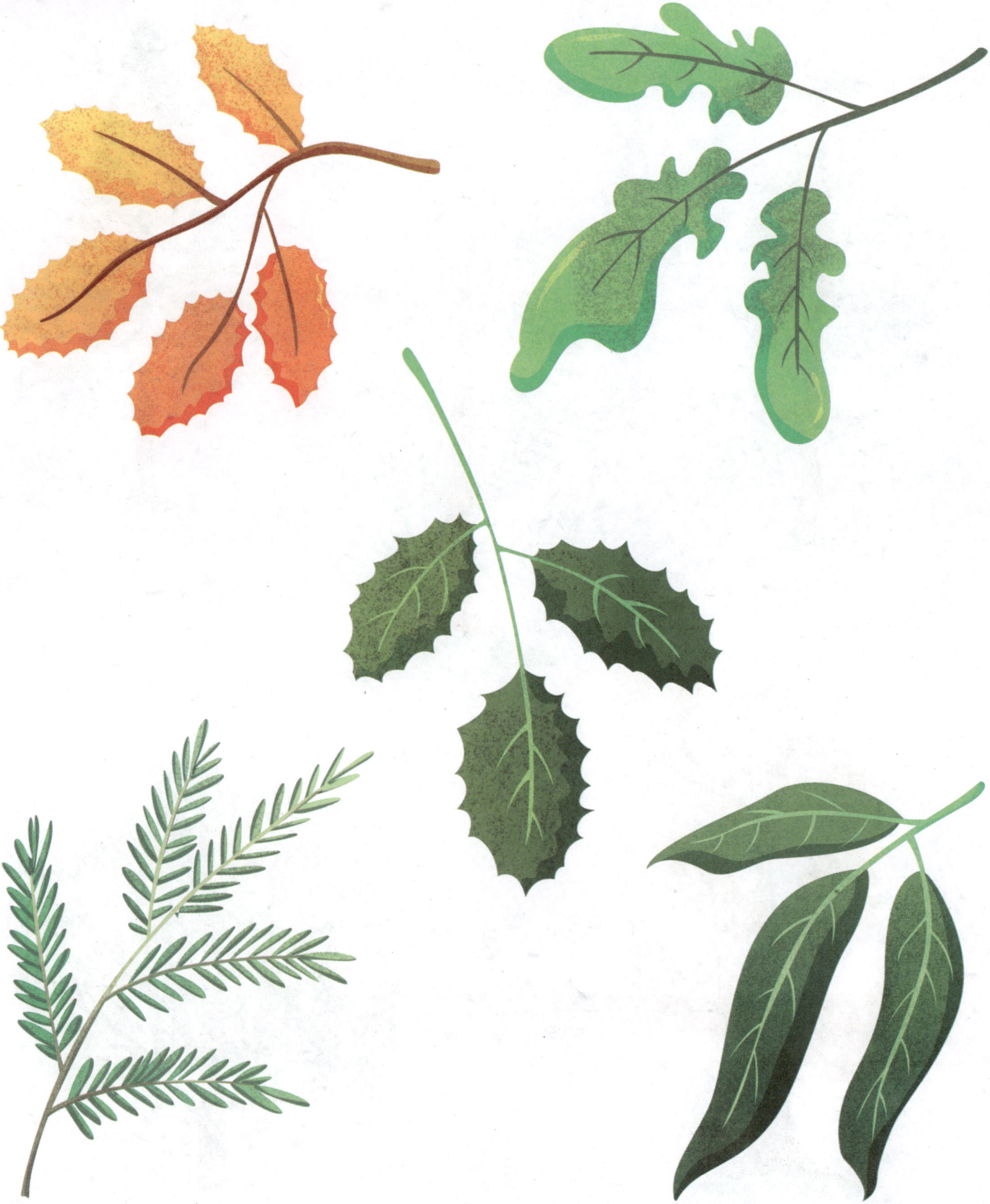

 Fill in the below blanks.

Plant that can stay on less water   CACT_S

Short tree   CED_R TREE

Tree having spiny leaves   H_LLY TREE

Long tree   KA_OK TREE

Conifer tree   LAR_H TREE

24

Help Adam find his way to the tree farm.

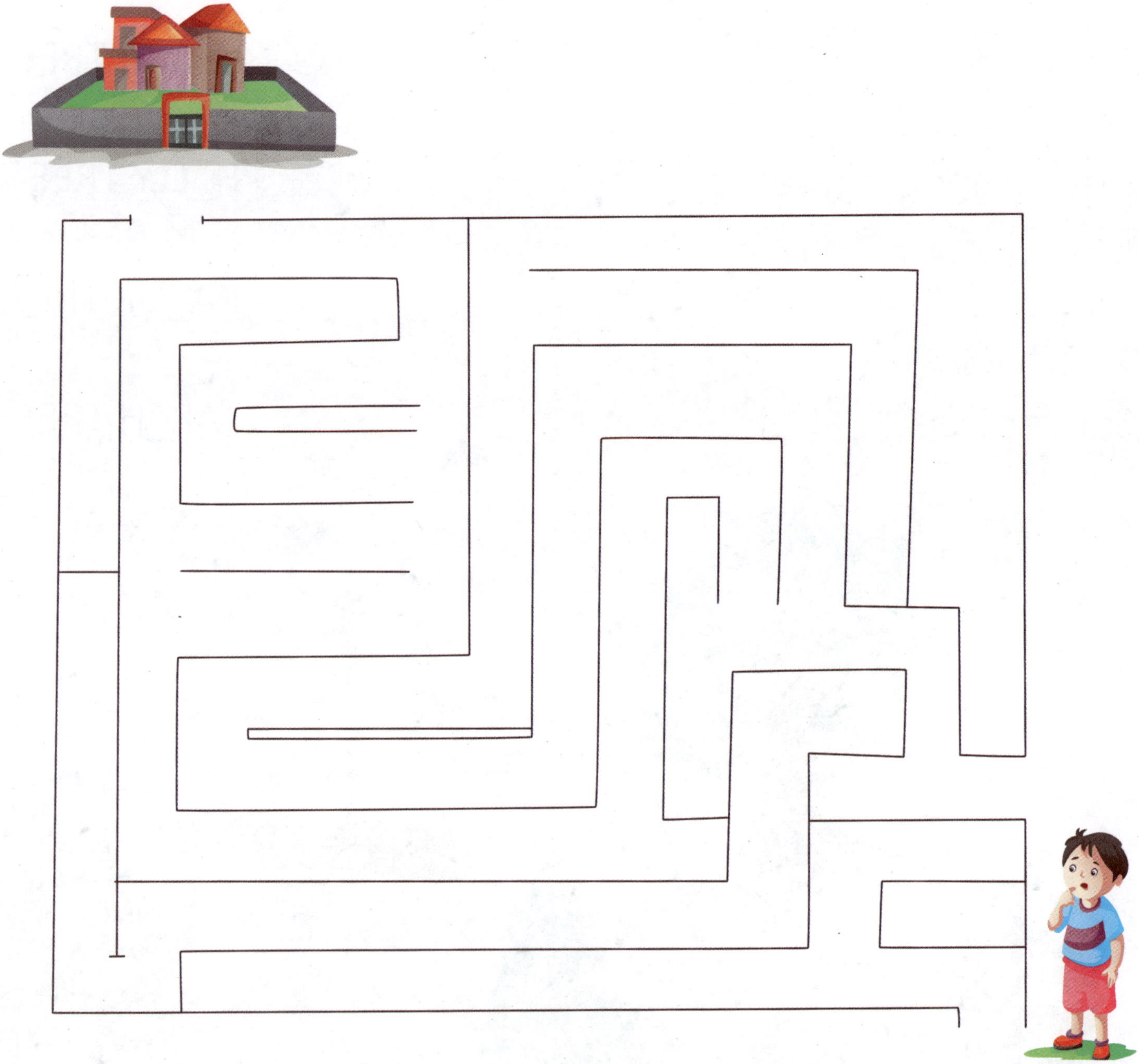

 Identify the below pictures and unscramble their names.

SISEHTNYSOTOHP

_____

TIURF

_____

REWOLF

_____

METS

_____

TOOR

_____

26 How to plant a tree.

Take some _____ 🟫 and put it into a _____ 🪴.

Make a _____ 🕳️ in the middle of the soil with your _____ ✋.

Drop some _____ 🌰 into the _____ 🕳️.

Now cover the _____ 🌰 with _____ 🟫.

Pour adequate _____ 💦 into the _____ 🪴.

Keep the _____ 🏺 in _____ ☀️.

After some days, a _____ 🌱 will grow.

Circle the things that plants need to grow.

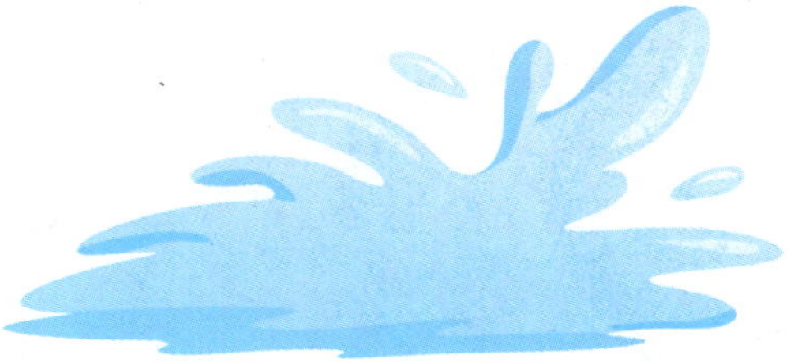

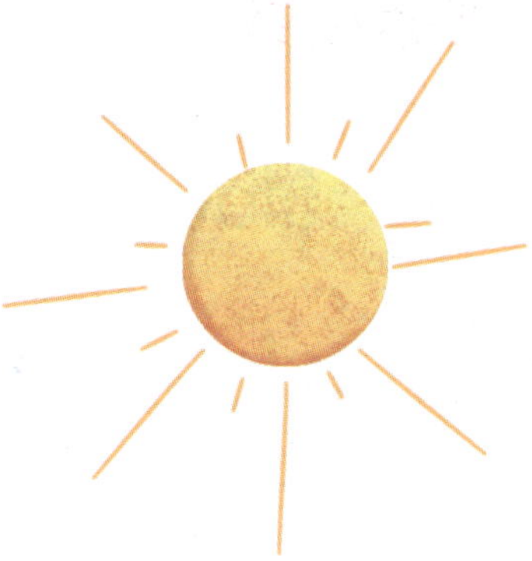

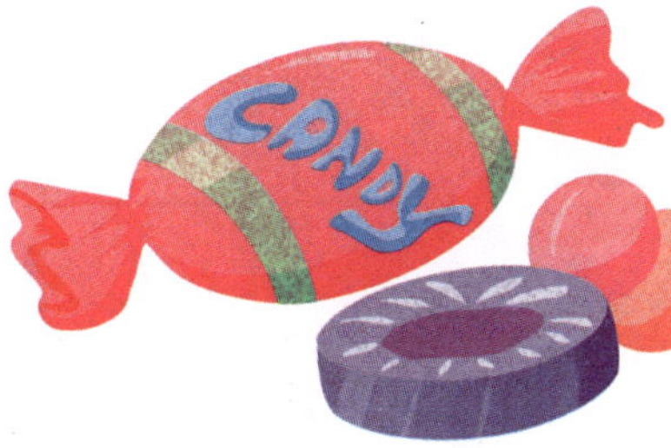

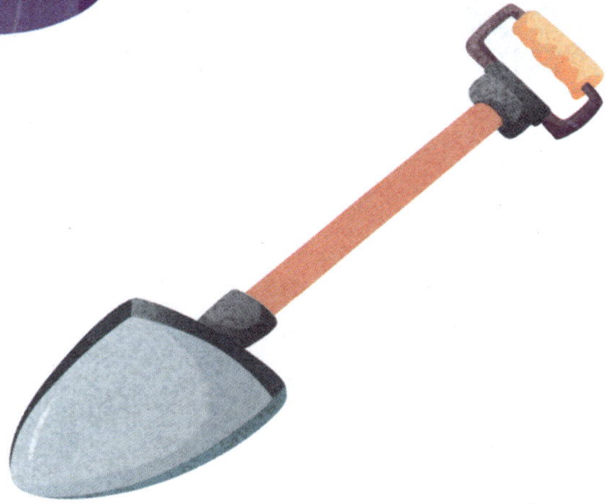

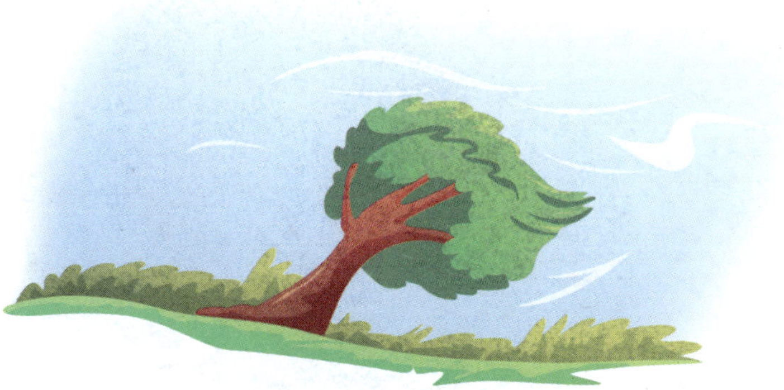

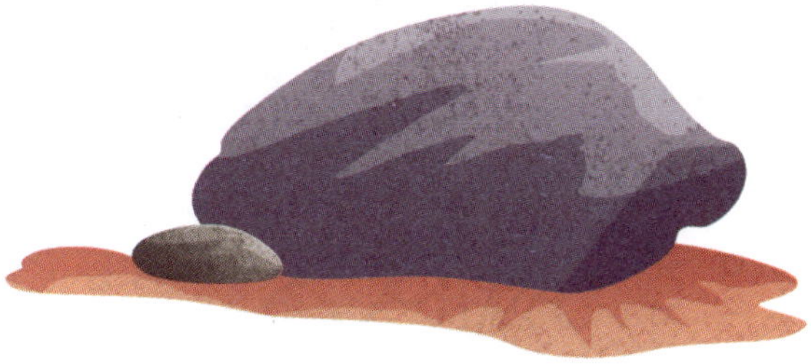

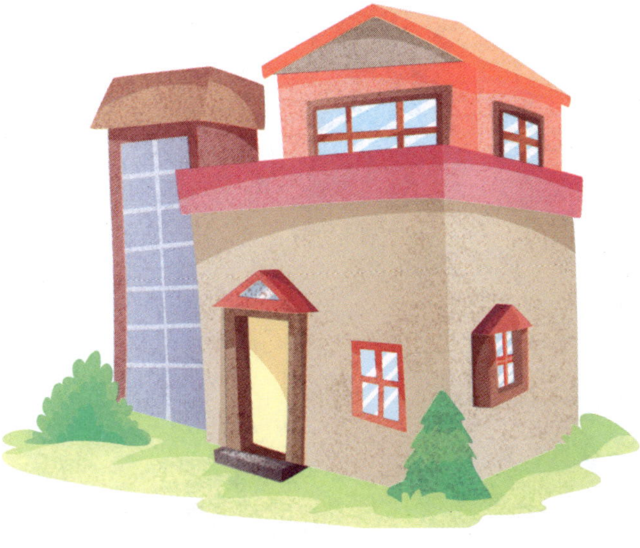

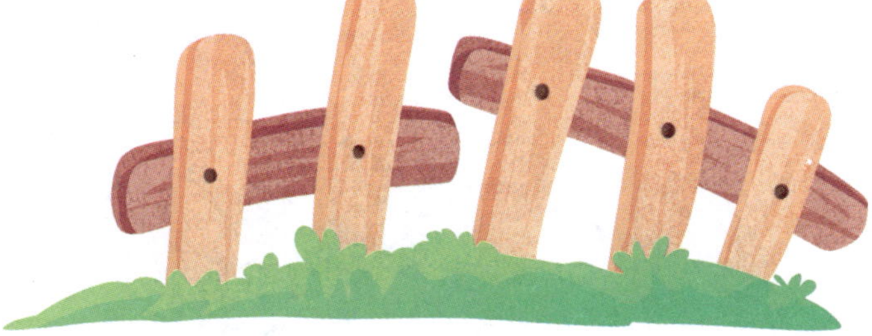

 Fill in the blanks and colour the tree with its respective colours.

The colour of branch is _____

The colour of roots is _____

The colour of leaves is _____

The colour of trunk is _____

 Draw a tree with your thumb prints.

Note: Colour your both thumbs with green colour and stamp it on a paper. Now use brown coloured crayon or sketch pen to draw the branches and trunk of the tree.

30 Identify the pictures and fill in the blank spaces.

Tr_n_ P_l_ P_n_

Ca_tu_ L_av_s Al_e v_r_

M_sh_oo_ R_o_s

Find out the differences.

32 Colour some thermocol beads with red colour to show apples. Now stick the beads on the tree.

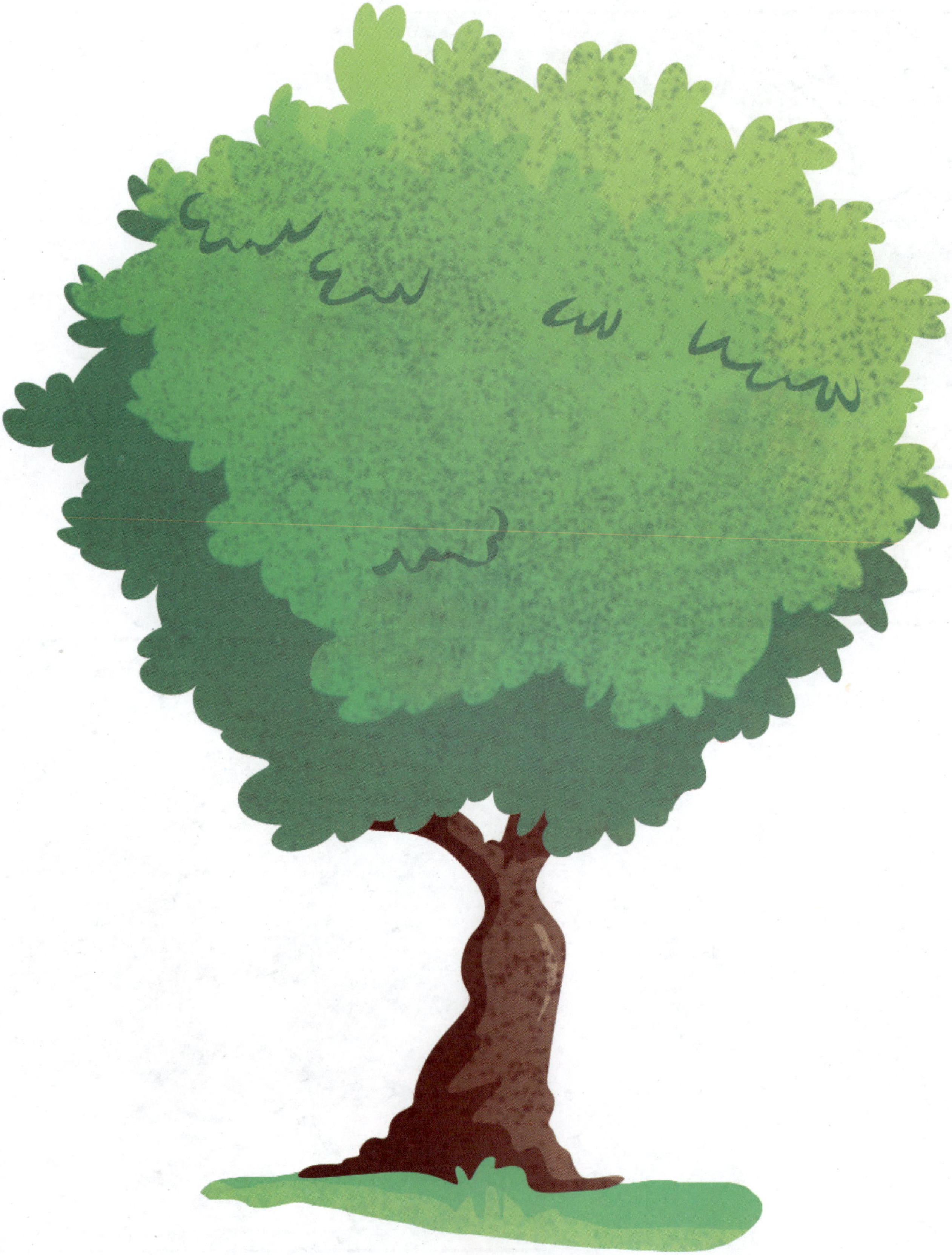

33 Tick the trees that can be grown in a garden.

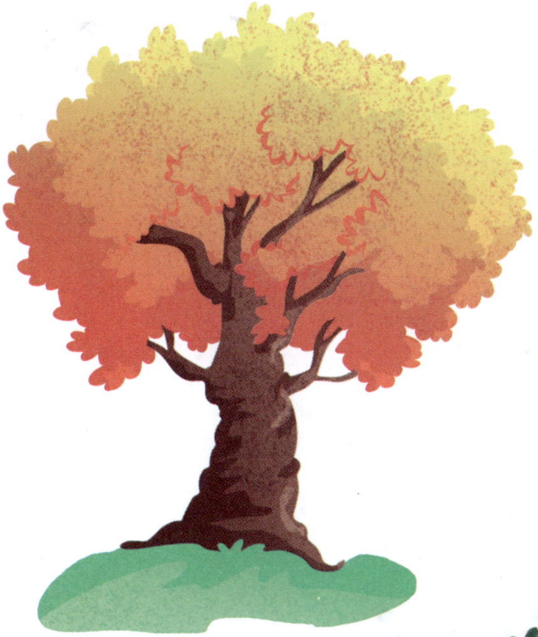

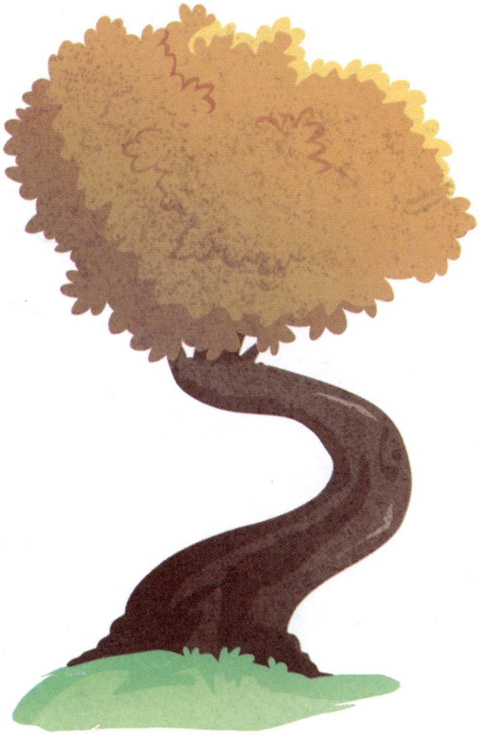

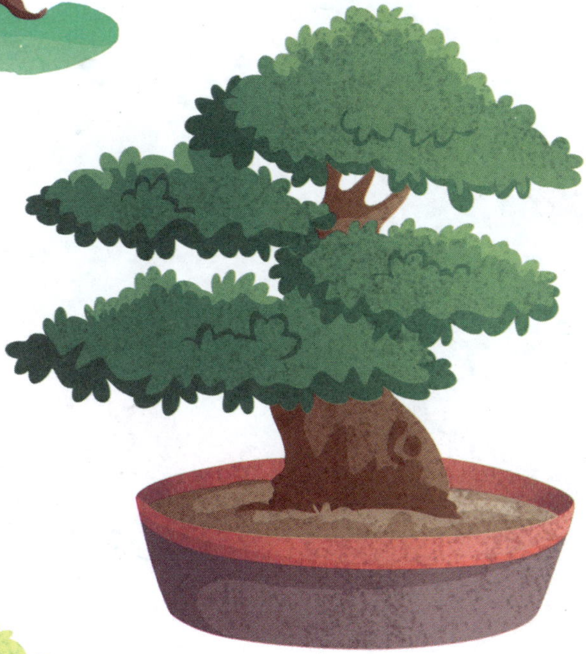

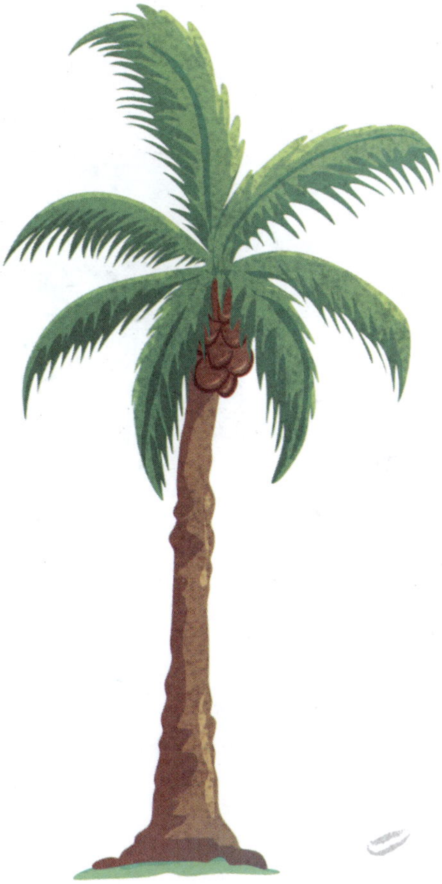

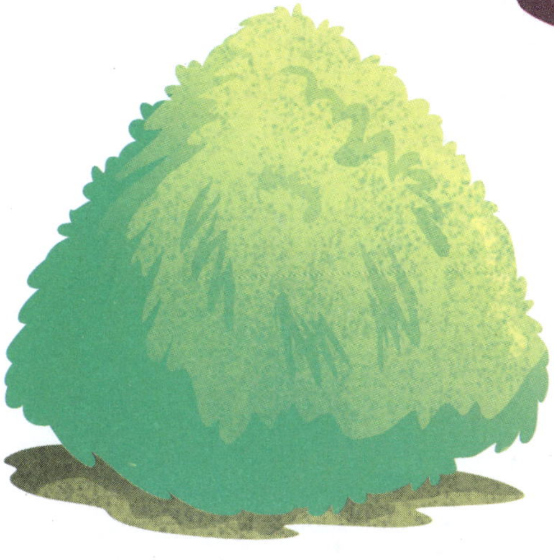

34 It's Christmas. Decorate this Christmas tree with various ornaments.

35 Complete the conversation between a tree and a plant.

Plant: Hey, TR_E. You are so big.

Tree: Yes, I am. I am older than you.

Plant: Wow! I too want to be as BI_ as you.

Tree: You'll surely be after sometime. Most PL_NTS grow into TRE_S.

Plant: Hurrah! I too will be big. Thank you!

Tree: You're welcome little one.

36 Tick the fruits that grow on plants and not on trees.

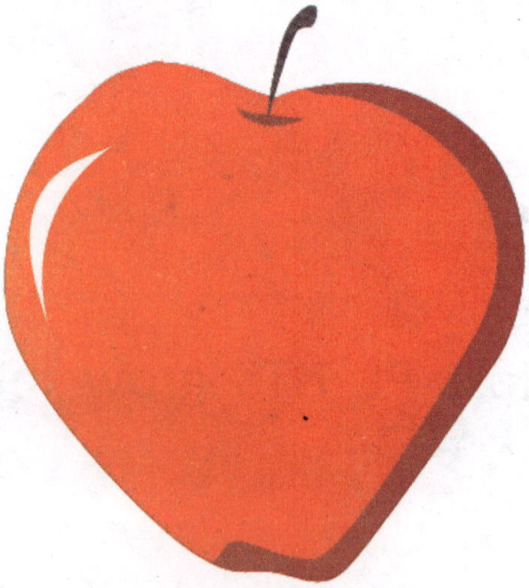
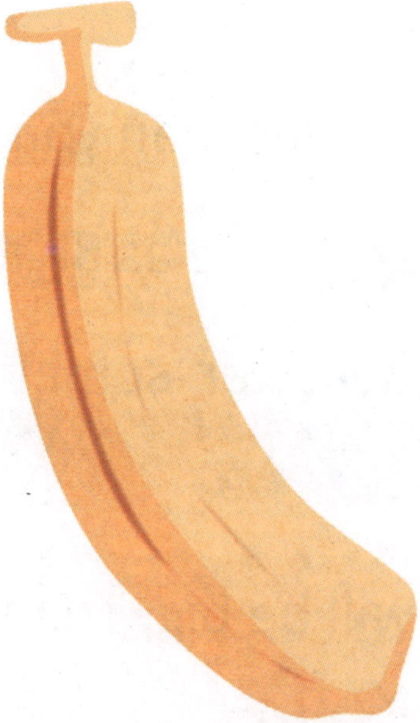
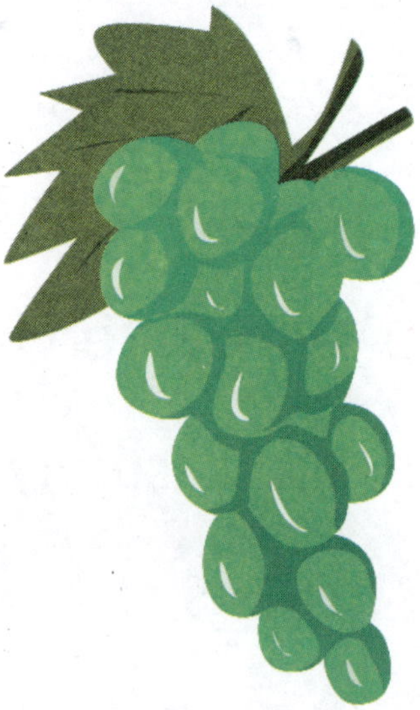
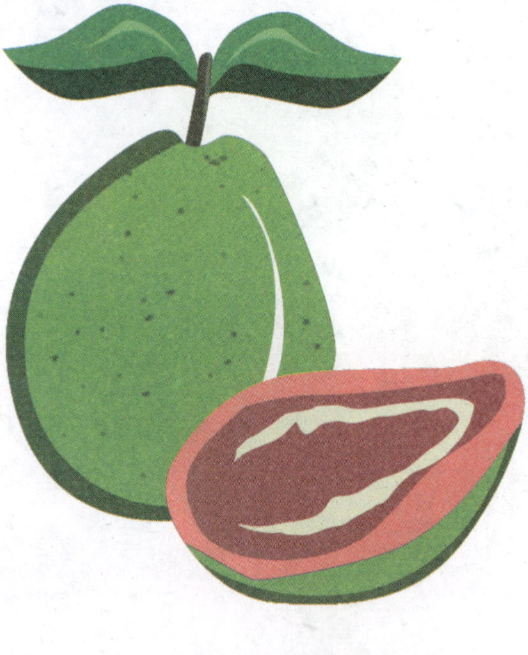
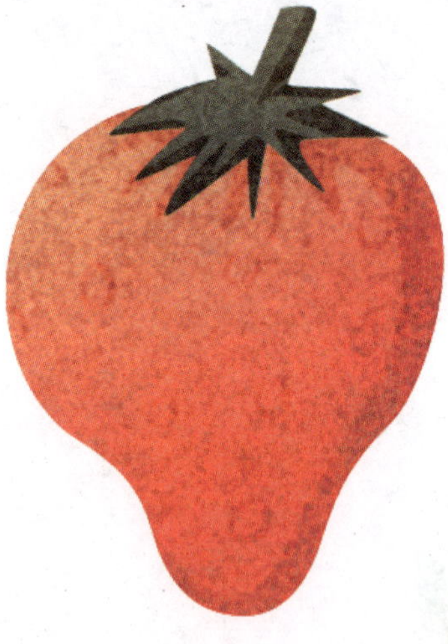
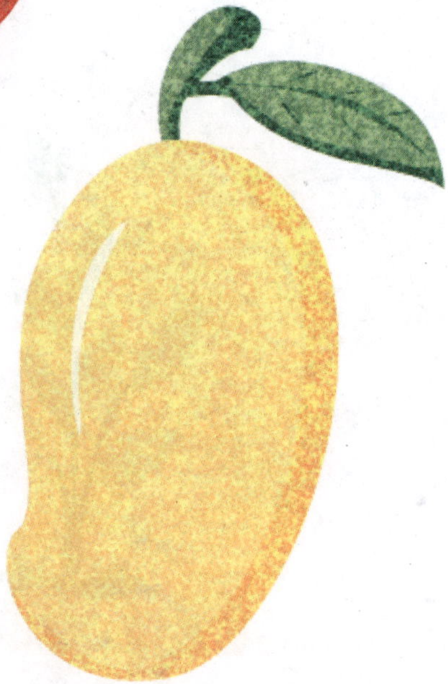
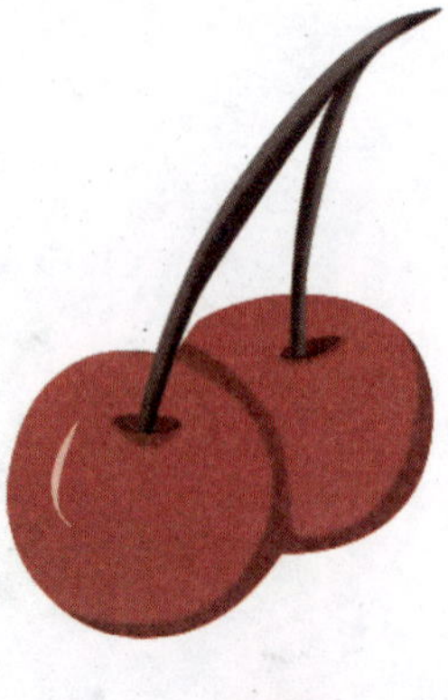

37 Circle plants and trees.

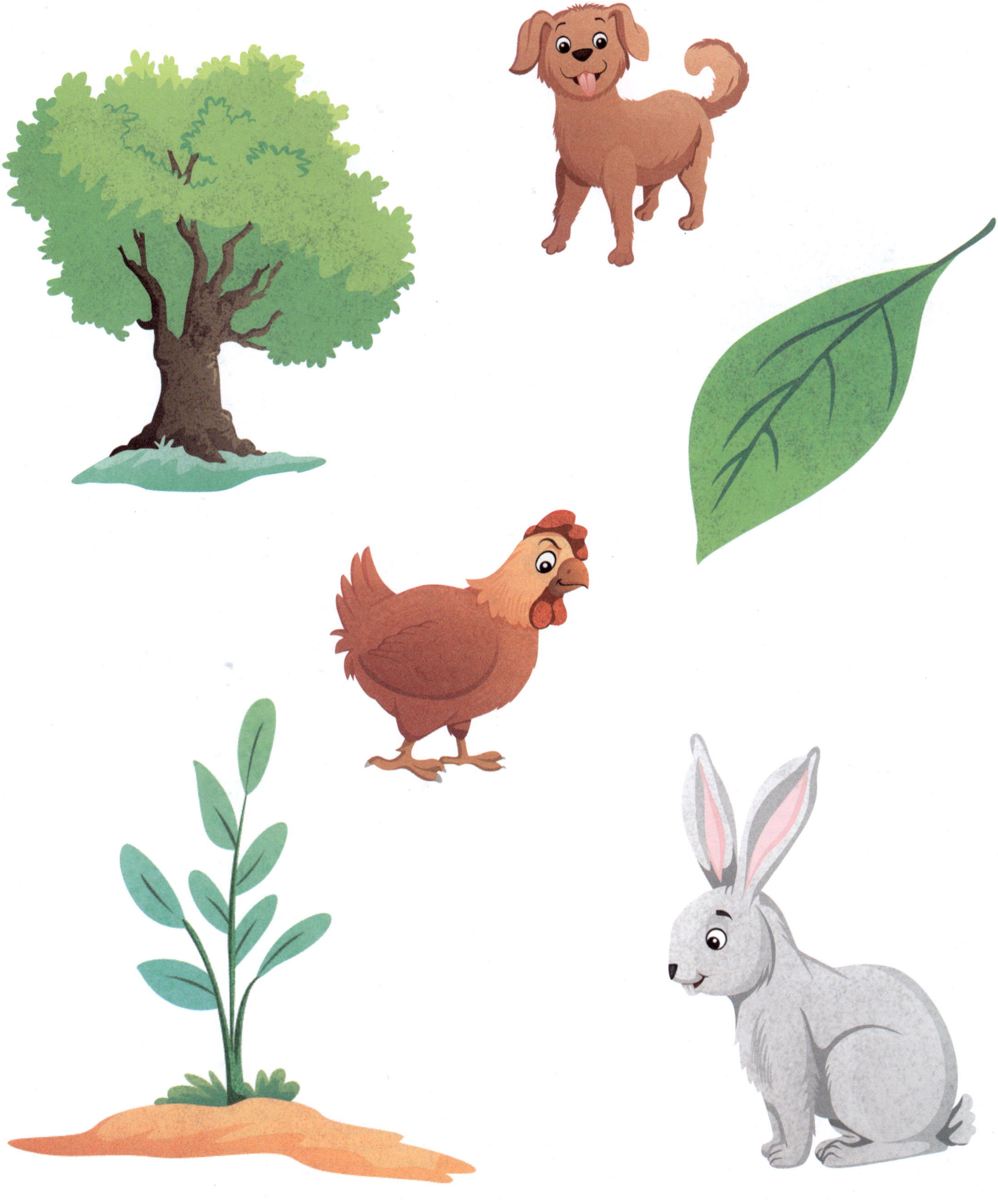

38 Complete the words that are used for tree plantation.

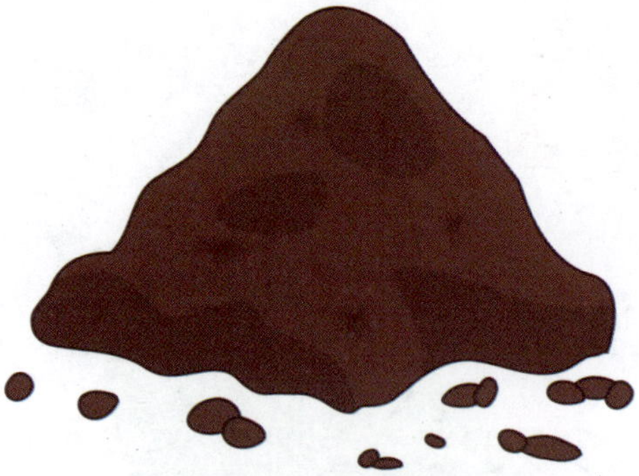

S_IL

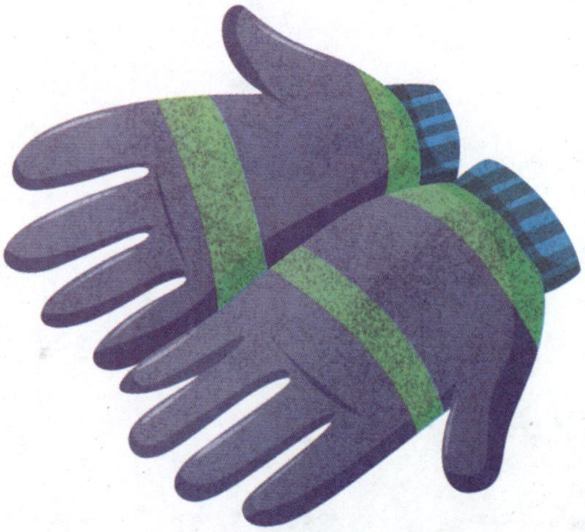

GLO_ES

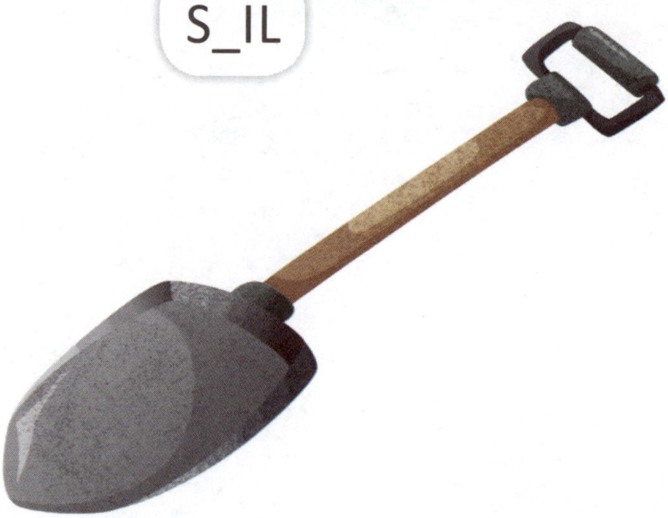

SPA_E

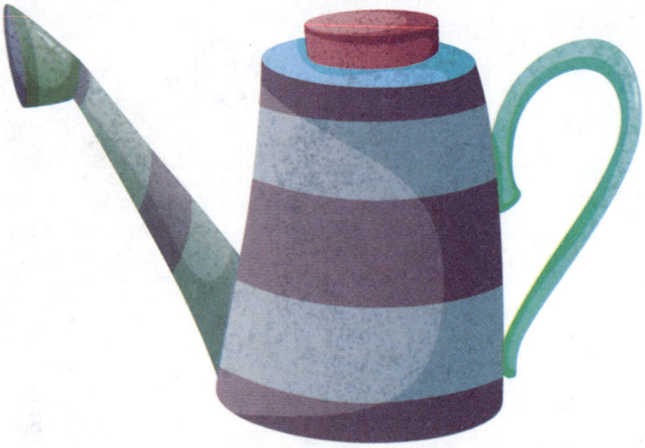

SPRINK_ER

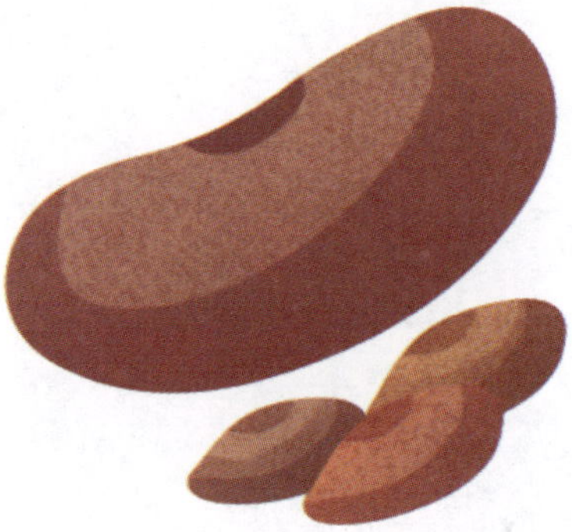

SE_DS

39 Lead the giraffe to the coconut tree.

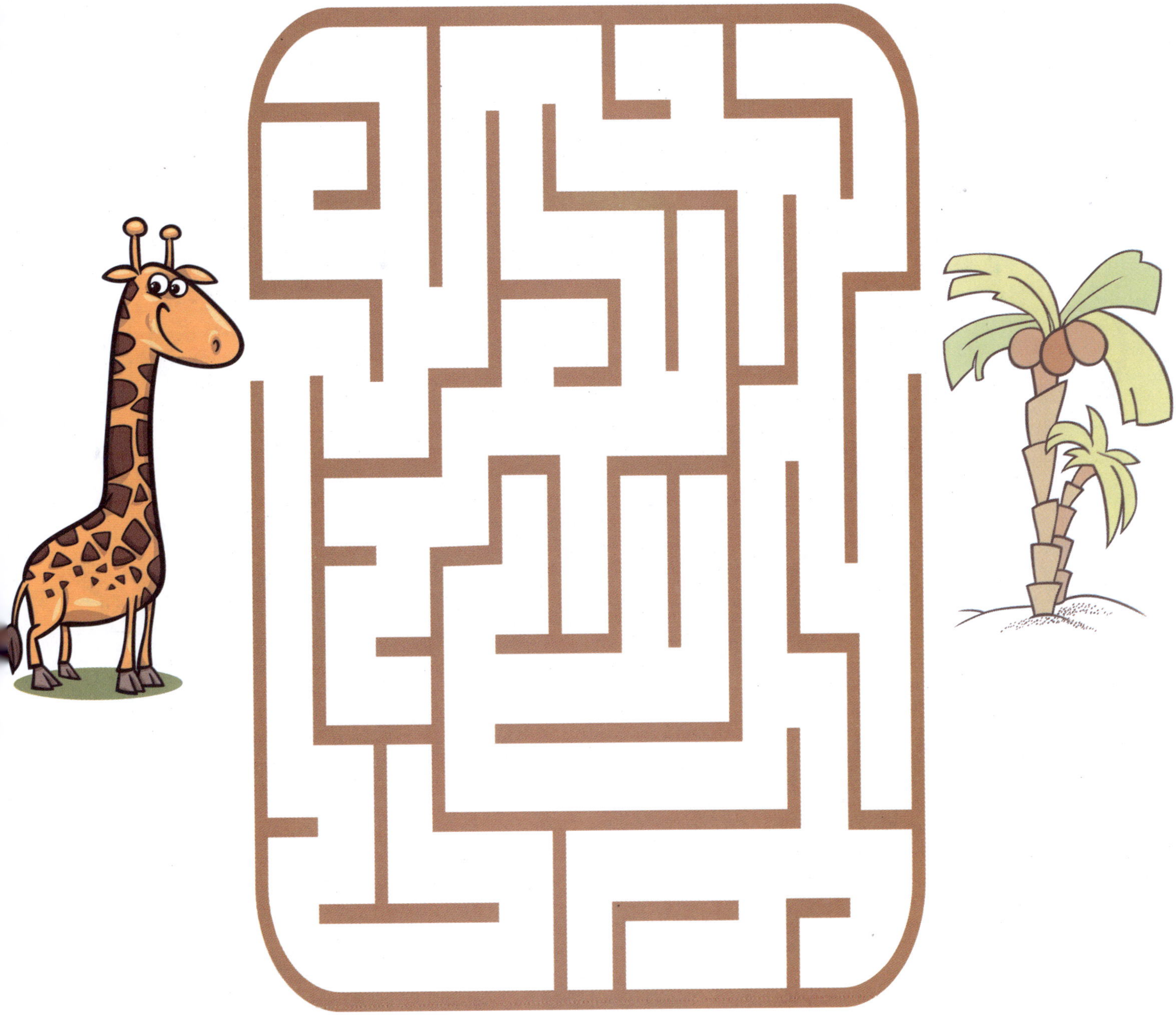

40 Circle the leafy vegetables.

CAB_AGE

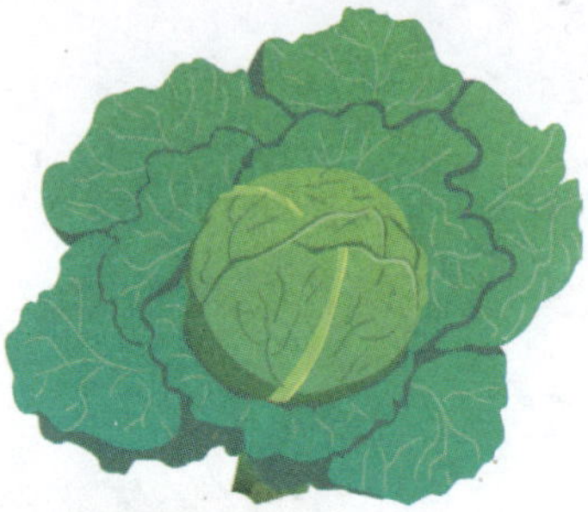

BROCC_LI

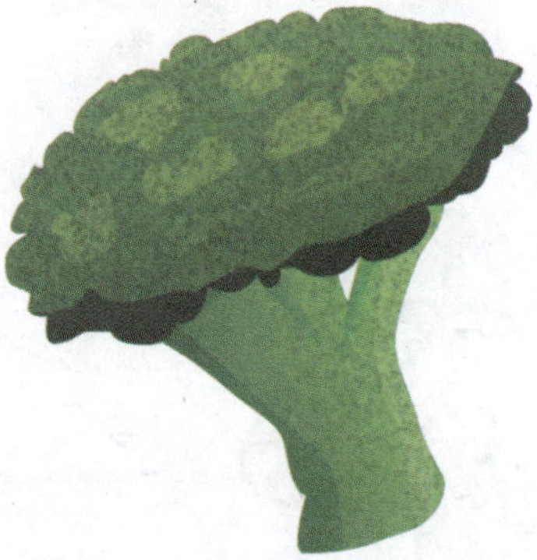

TU_NIP

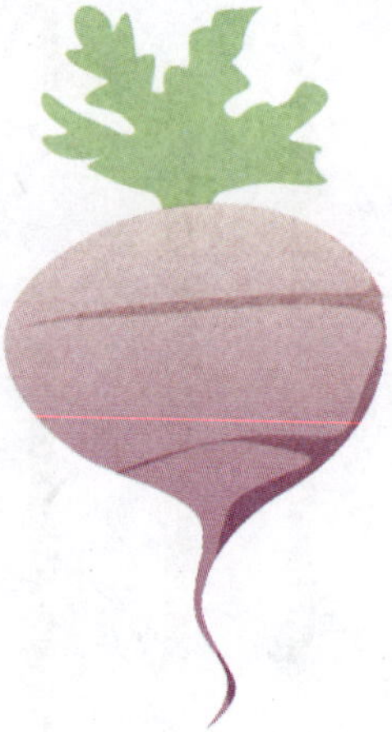

CAR_OT

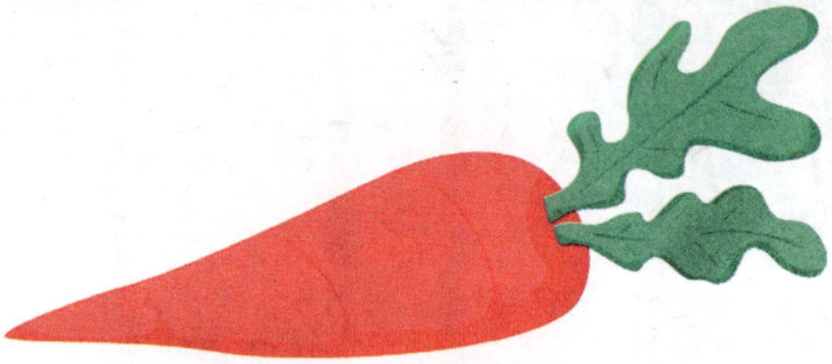

GOU_D

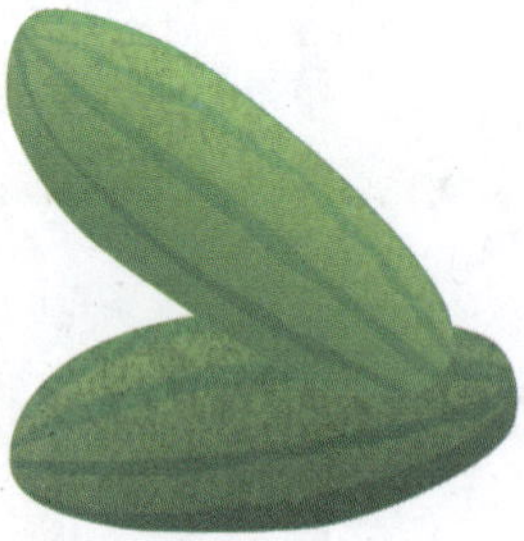

SP_NACH

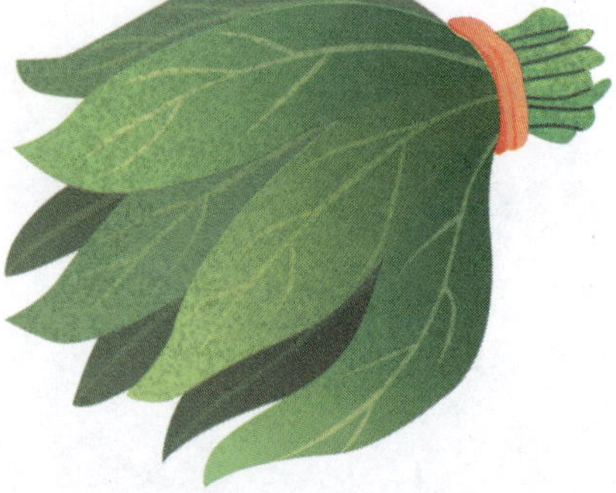

41 Draw a line from the word to its figure.

Leaf

Rose bush

Cactus

Tree

Palm tree

Mushroom

Look at the picture and fill the crossword with names of the pictures with corresponding numbers.

 Collect some leaves of different trees and outline them keeping them on the space provided below. Now colour them. Also write the name of the leaves beneath their pictures.

44 Shoot is the portion of the plant above the ground. We eat shoots of many plants. Circle the edible shoot plants.

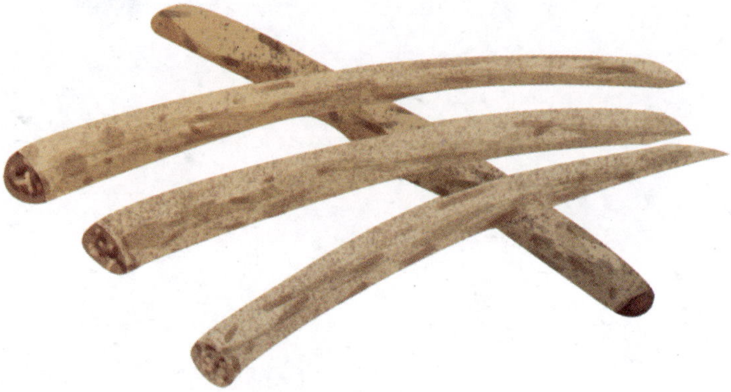

Trees give us many things. Some of their uses are listed below. Fill in the blank spaces to complete the word.

Trees give us W0_D

Trees give us OXY_EN

Trees provide us SHAD_

Trees give us MEDIC_NES

Trees give us FRU_T and VEGETA_LES to eat.

46 Fill up the blanks to complete the names of the medicinal plants given below.

ALE_ VERA

DANDEL_ON FLOWER

CHI_I PEPPER

MORIN_A PLANT

WHI_E WILLOW

HORSE CHES_NUT

OPIUM PO_PY

Given below is the life cycle of a plant. Fill in the blank spaces to complete the words.

PL_NTS grow from SEE_DS.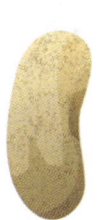

When a seed is planted, it first turns into a SEE_LING.

After sometime, the seedling grows into a PLA_T.

The plant then produces seeds which can grow more TR_ES.

48 Number the stages of the plant in order from beginning to end.

 There are certain plants that are used as spices. Identify the plants and match them with their respective names.

Clove

Cinnamon

Pepper

Black Cardamom

Cassia

Coriander seeds

Fennel seeds

50 Colour the tree plantation activity.

51 Trees and plants grow when seeds travel from one place to another. Complete the below sentences to know how seeds travel.

Seeds travel by WIN_.

Seeds travel by WAT_R.

Seeds transfer through ANIM_LS.

Seeds grow when planted by HUMA_S.

Seeds disperse by BURST_NG.

52 Complete the names of edible flower plants.

BA_IL

CLOV_R

BROCCO_I

MI_T

OREG_NO

RO_E

CA_LIFLOWER

MAR_GOLD

Plants and trees give us fibre to produce clothes. Given below are the plants and some fabrics. Match the plant with the fibre it produces.

linen

sisal

kenaf

cotton

jute

coir

54 Circle the climbing plants.

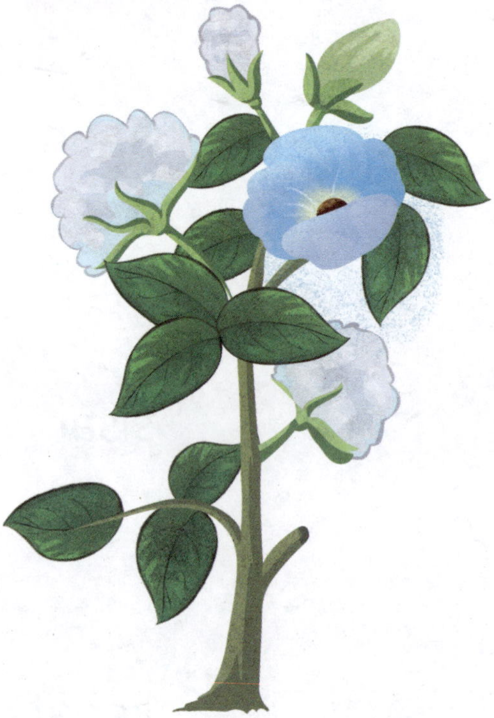

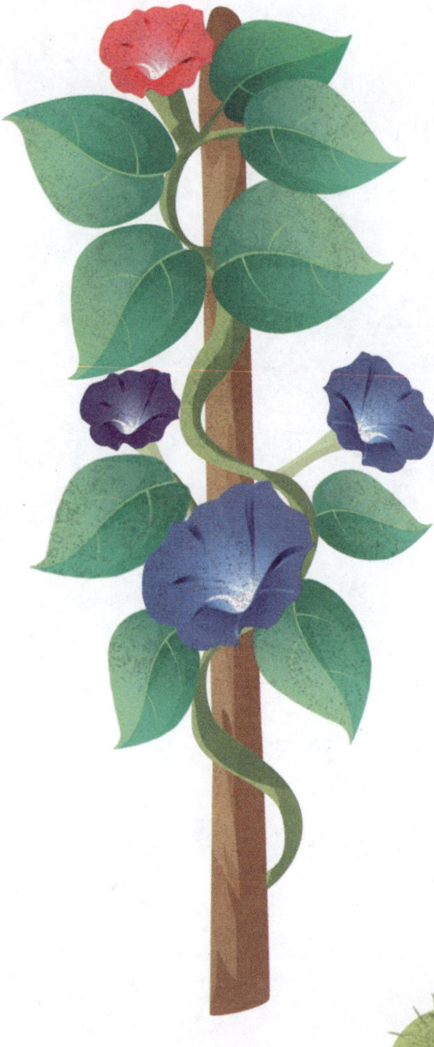

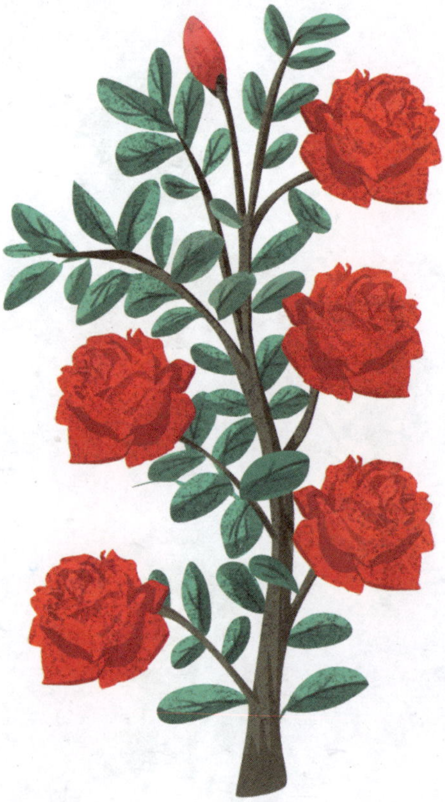

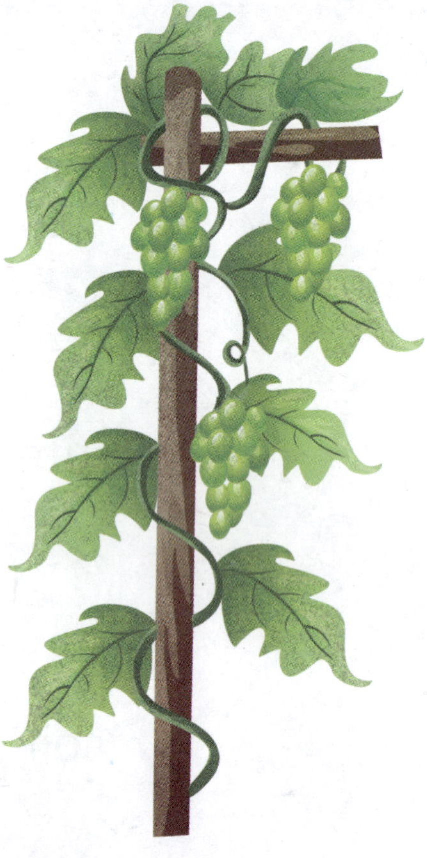

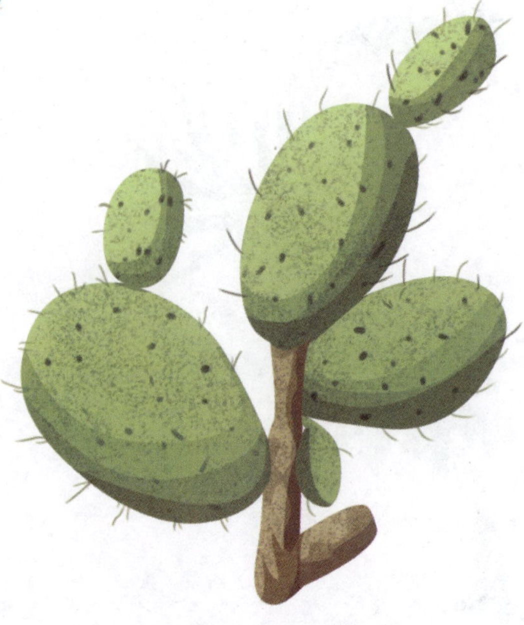

55

Follow the dots to complete the picture.

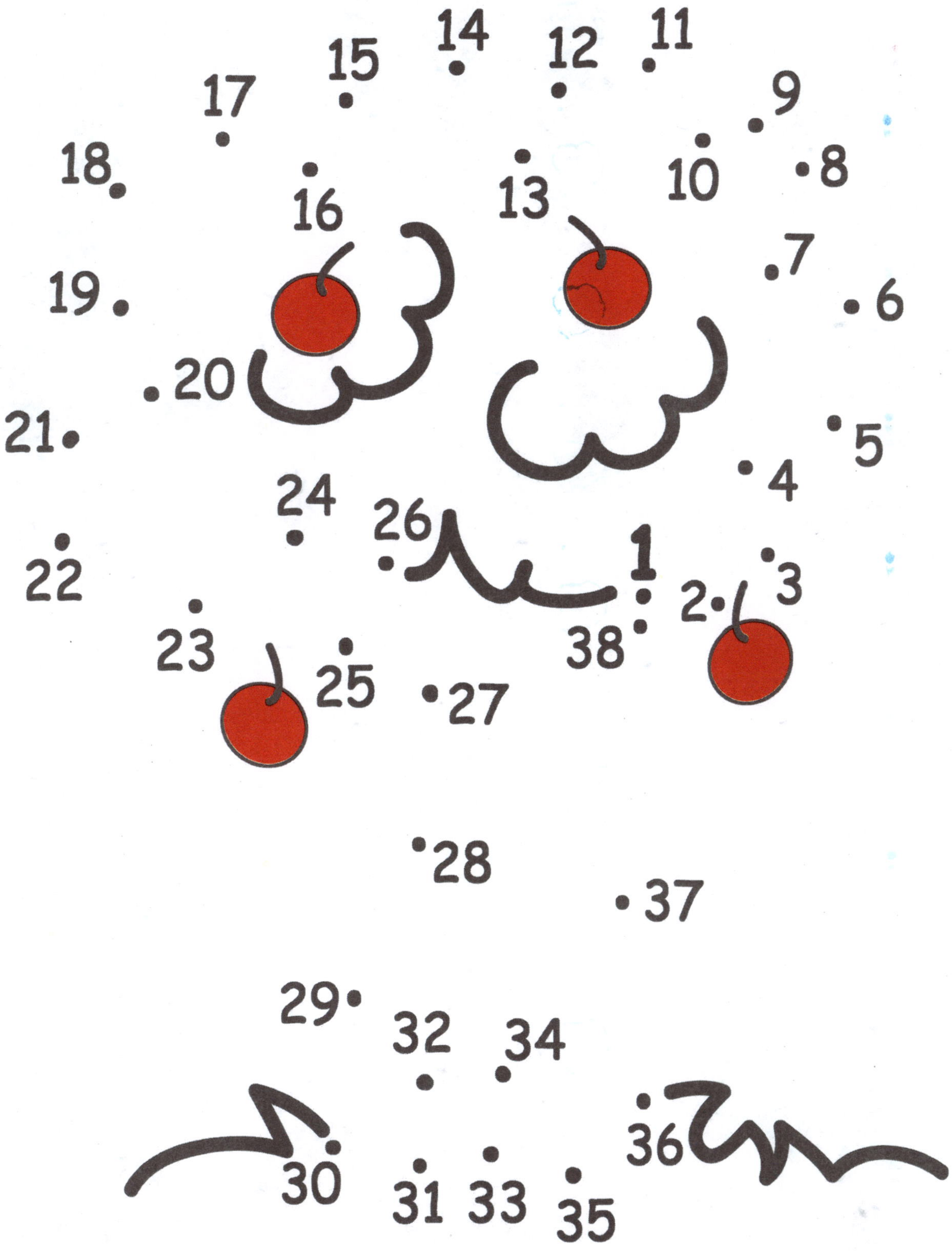

56 Tick those trees that do not bear fruits.

57 Reach the end to save trees from cutting down.

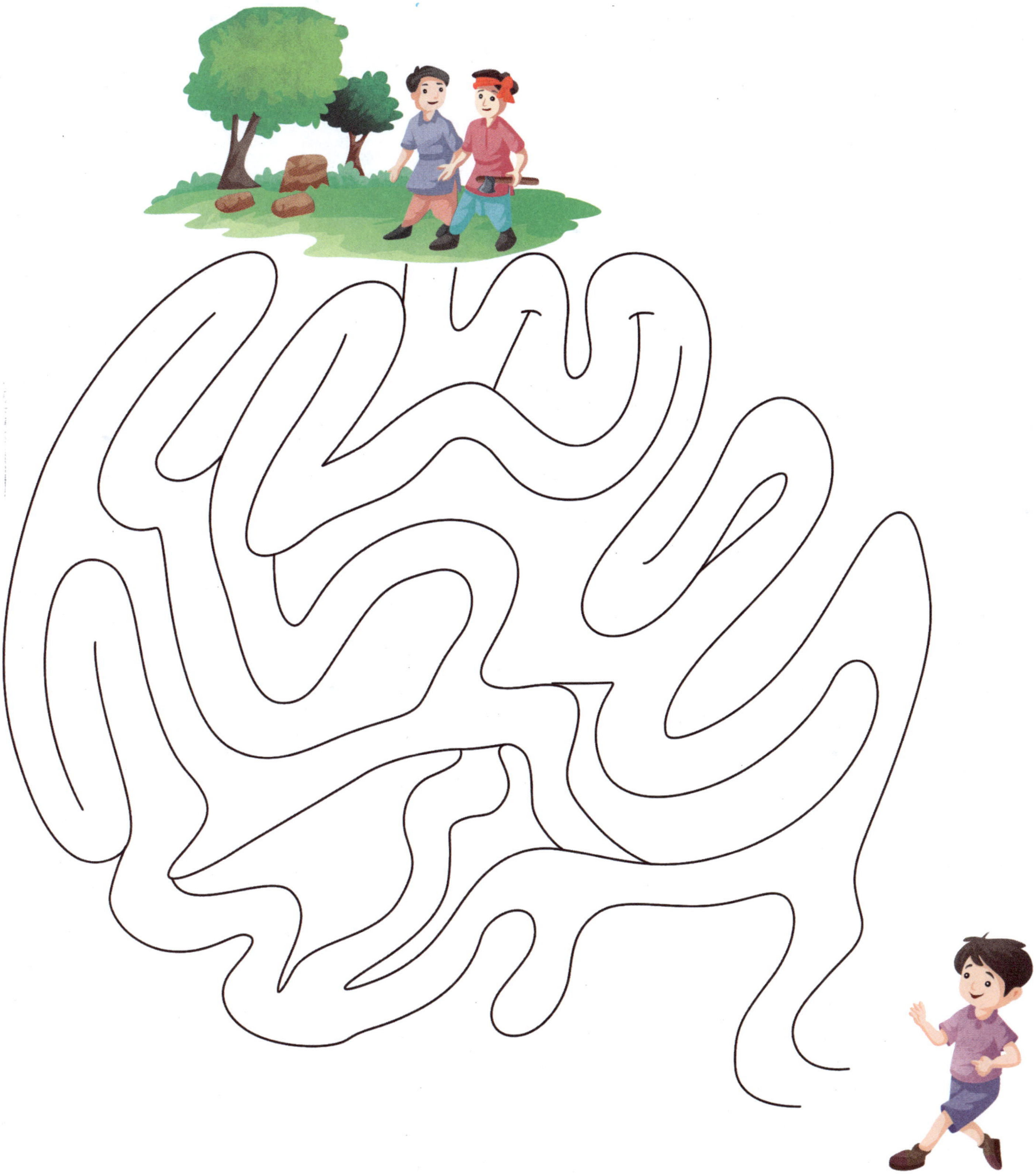

Make a tree with various types of seeds.

Complete the names of the below plants by filling up the blanks.

CLO_ER

OREG_NO

CREEPI_G THYME

VIO_ETS

MI_T

 Number the pots correctly to complete the plant lifecycle.

61 Here are some shade trees. Pick the correct answer and tick them. Put a cross against those which are not.

62 Spot the differences between the below two pictures.

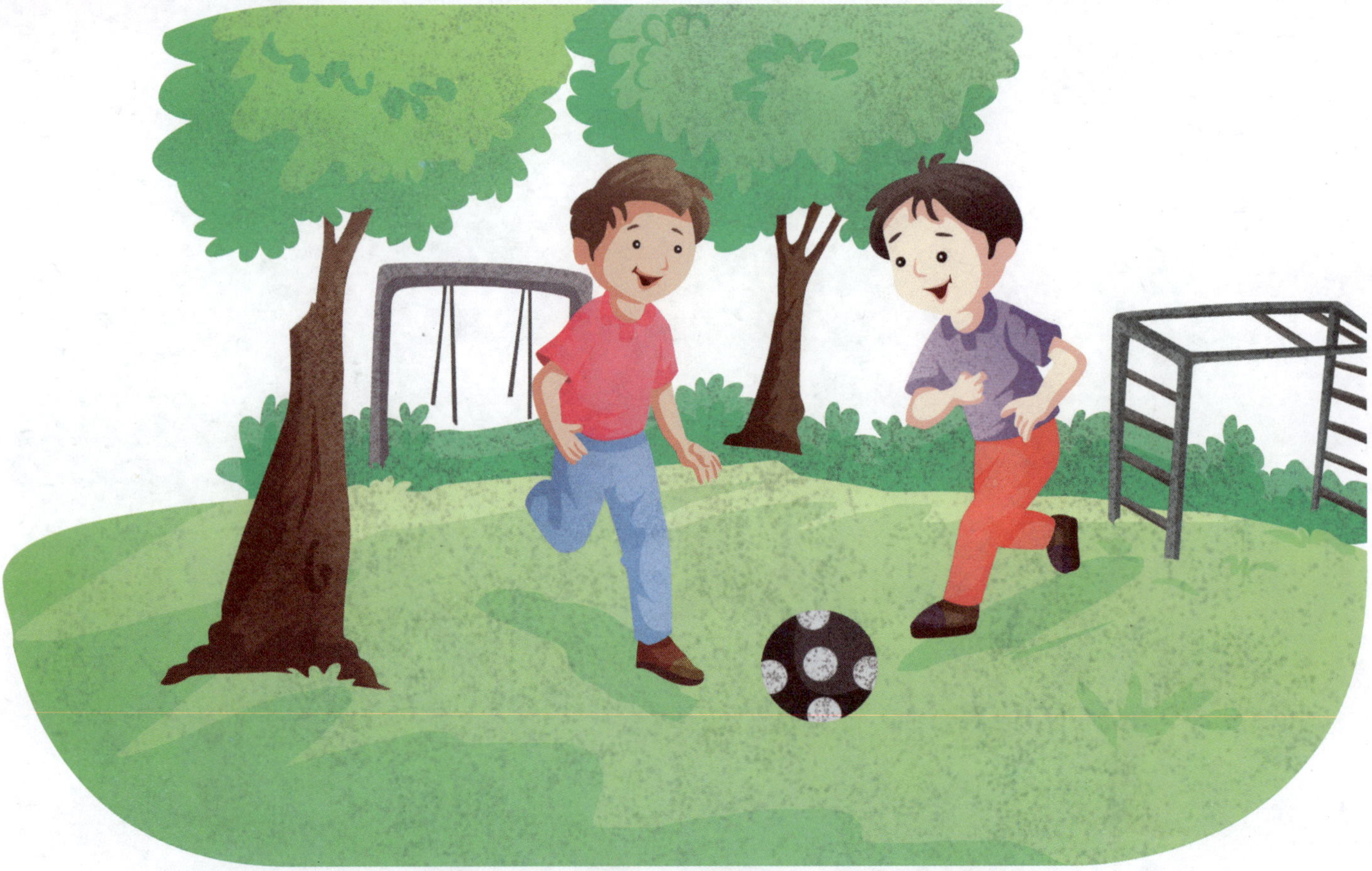

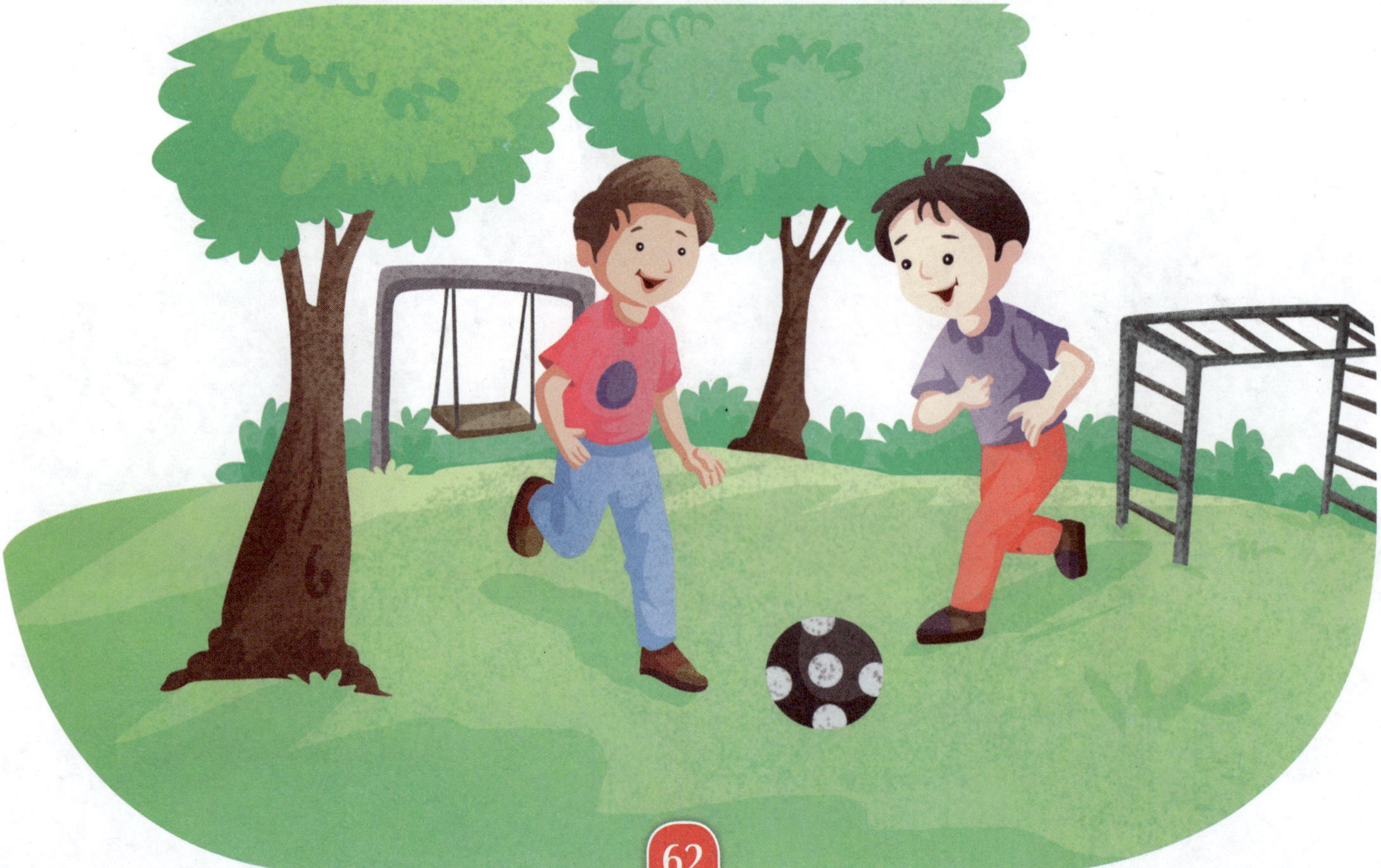

63 Trees are covered with snow in winter season. Depict the same by sticking cotton on trees and complete the picture.

64 Sunflower is unique in its characteristic that it faces the sun. Draw some more sunflowers as the sun is shining.

Touch-me-not plant folds itself inward when touched. Complete the picture of the plant as the kid has touched its leaves.

66 Take a small leaf. Keep it on a paper and outline it. Now cut it as per its shape and colour it brown. Now make many more leaves in the same way. Then paste these leaves on the tree below to make it an autumn tree.

67 Match the different types of plant with their pictures.

Shrubs

Herbs

Climbers

Creepers

Thorny plants

Water plants

68

Below leaf is labeled. Fill in the blanks and complete the names of its parts.

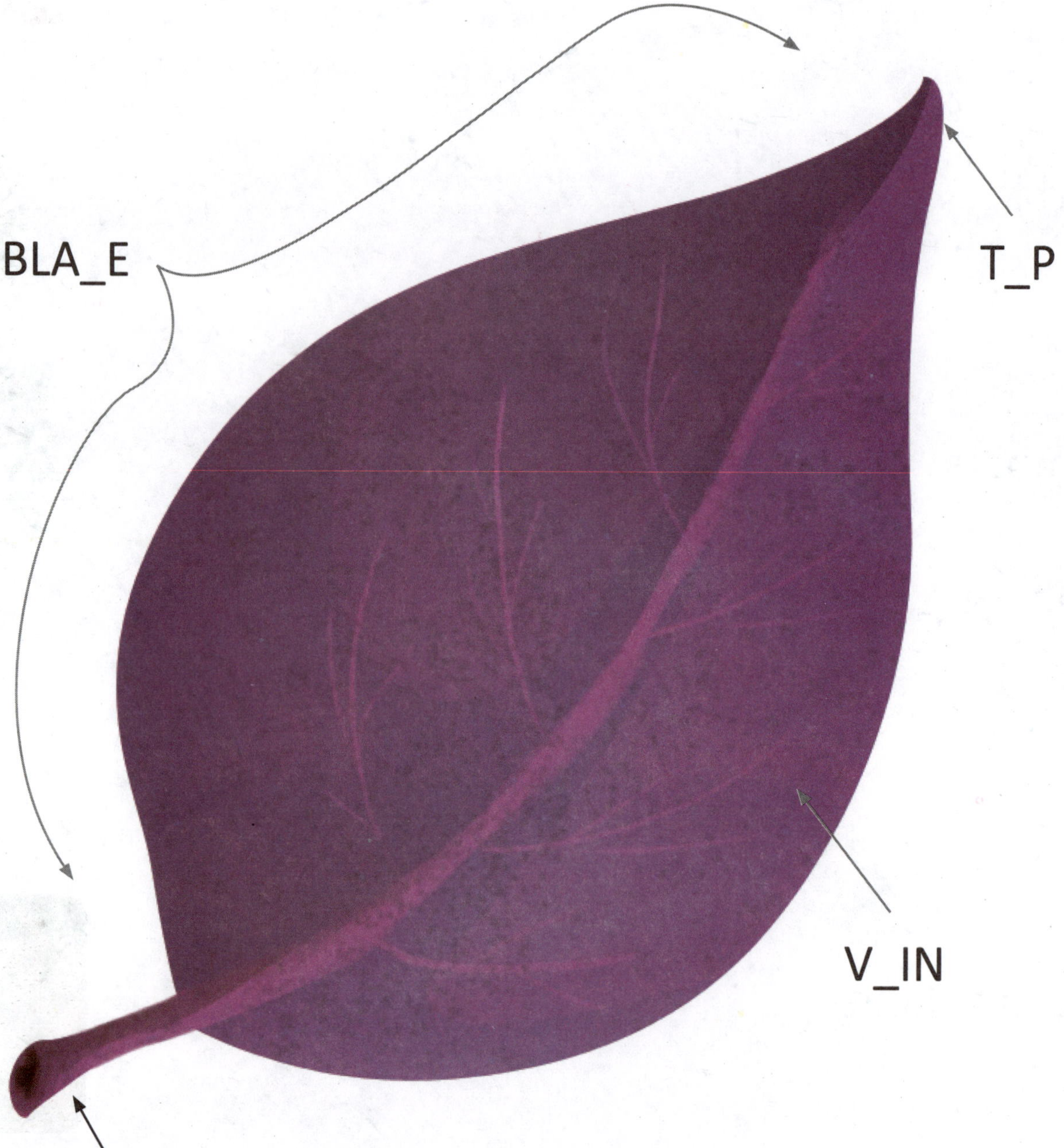
BLA_E
T_P
V_IN
STA_K

69 Decorate the Christmas tree with colourful thermocol balls.

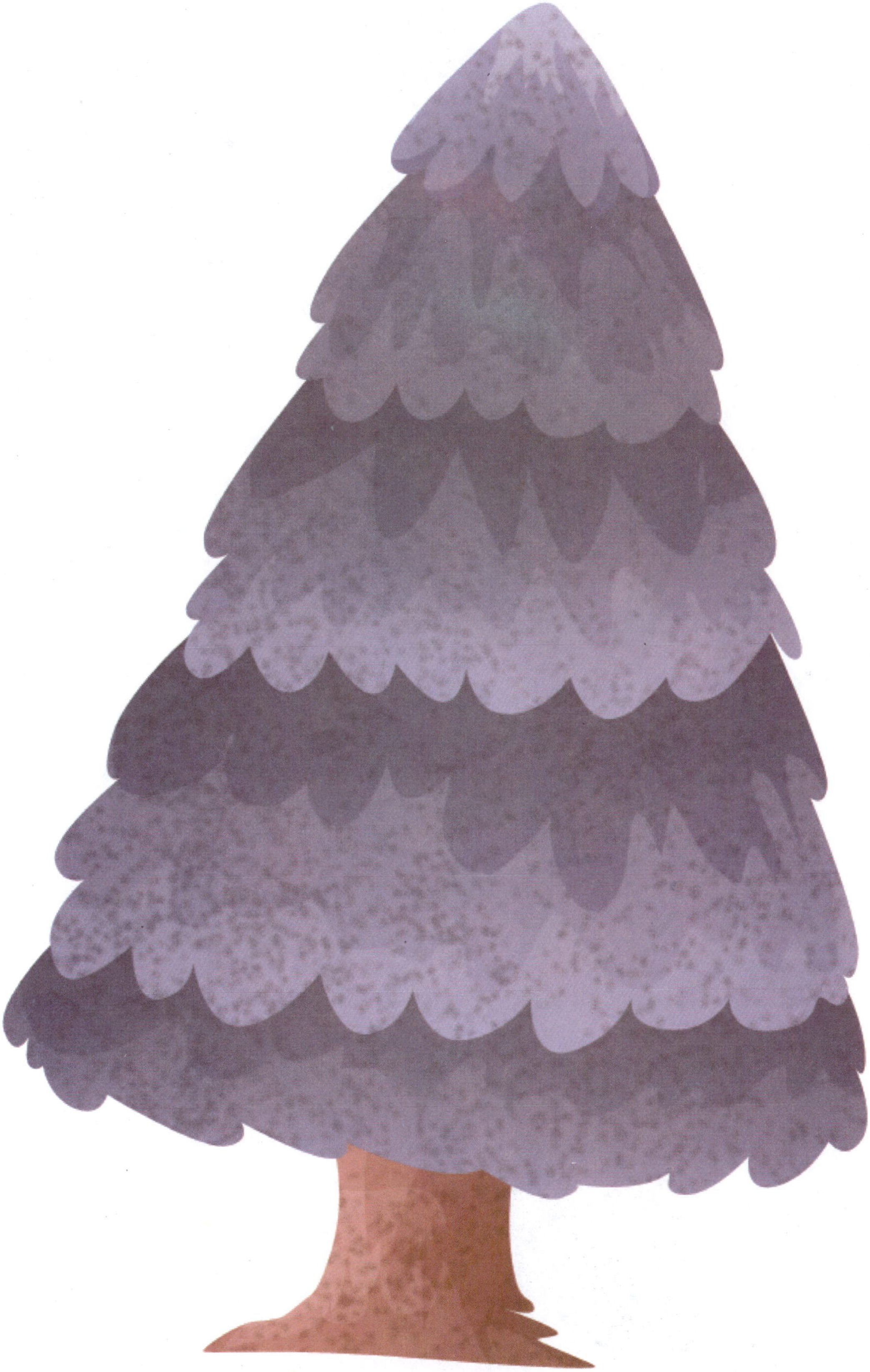

70

Stick buttons of different colours as shown in the picture to show the leaves.

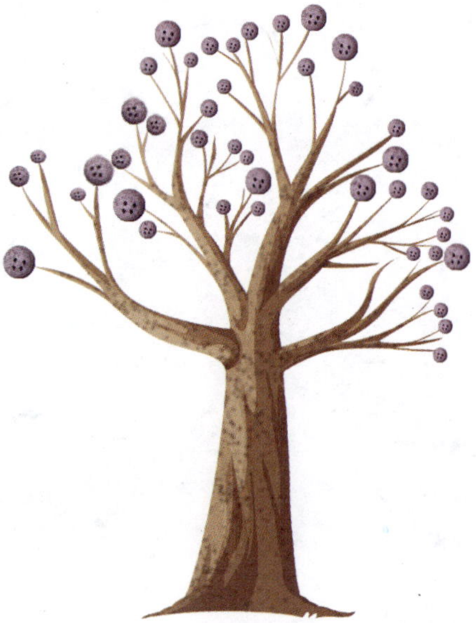

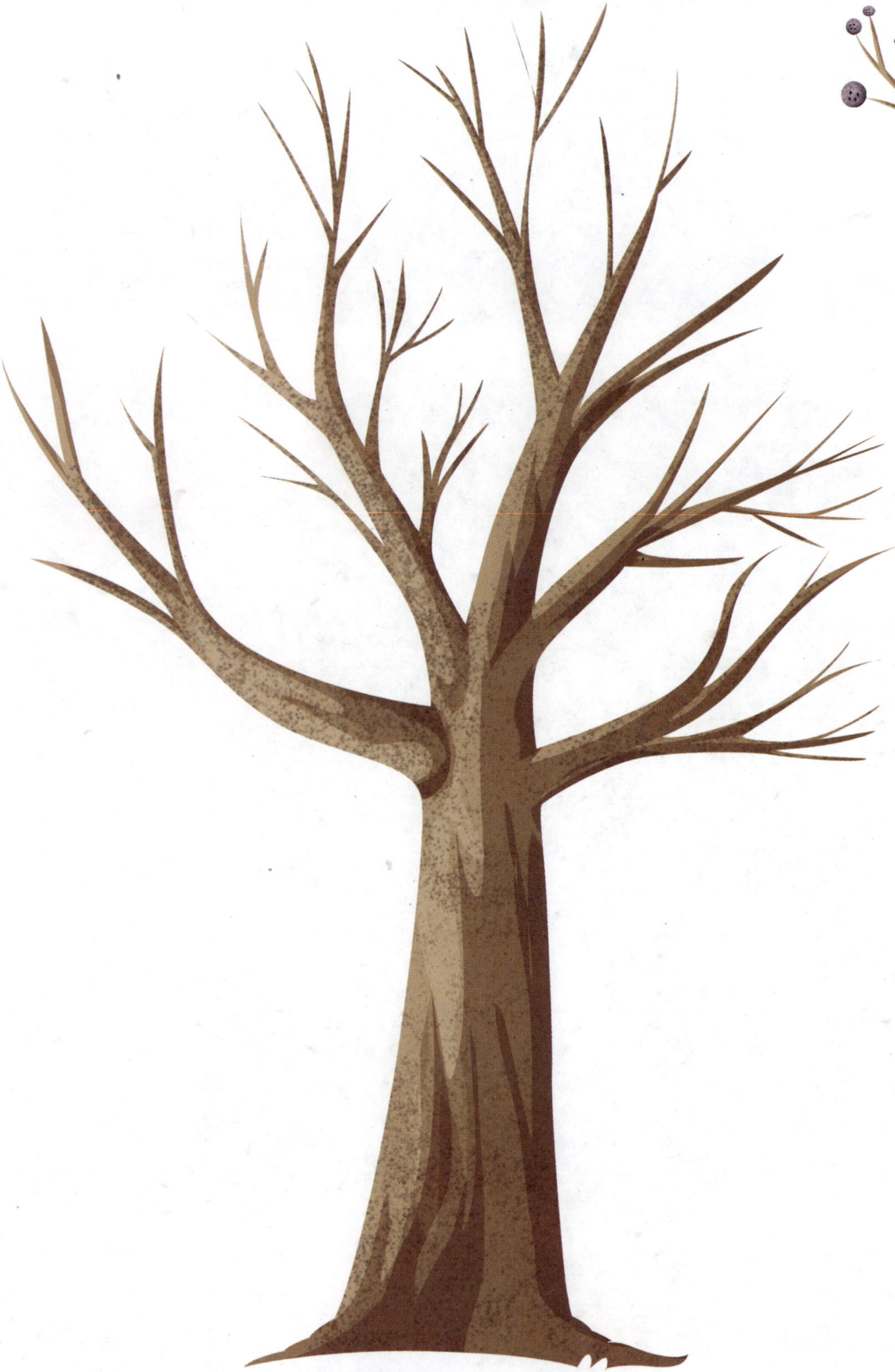

71 Draw a line to match the parts of the tree with their names given in the box below.

Trunk \ Crown \ Branches \ Leaf \ Fruit

72 Take a big leaf, make its outline keeping it on a paper. Now draw the veins of the leaves and colour it. Now, your leaf is ready.

73 Colour the below leaves.

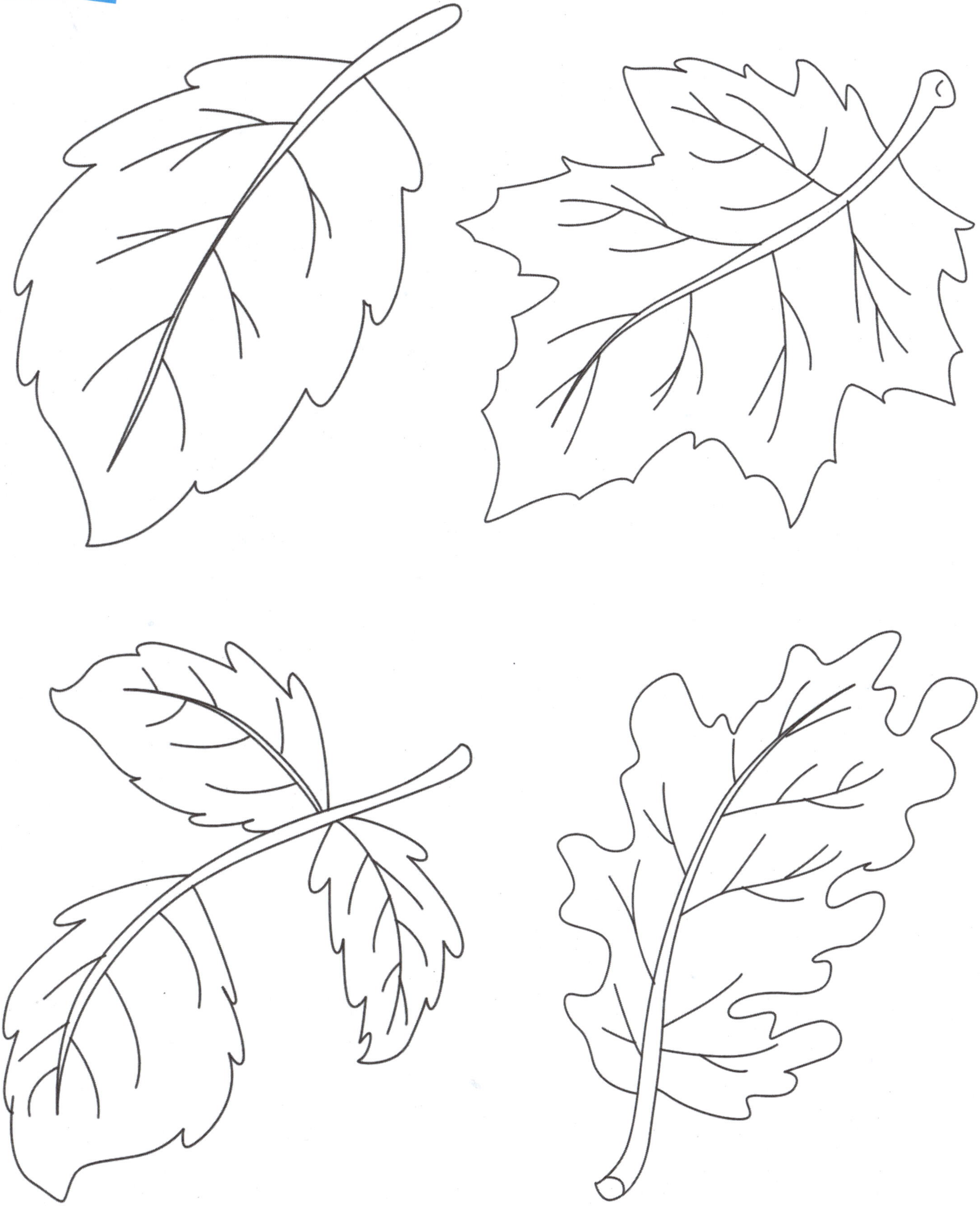

Knowing parts of a leaf.

Colour the veins green

Colour the stalk brown

Colour the tip red

Colour the blade dark green

 Collect and paste different leaves to make a collage.

Fill in the maple leaf with seeds of your choice

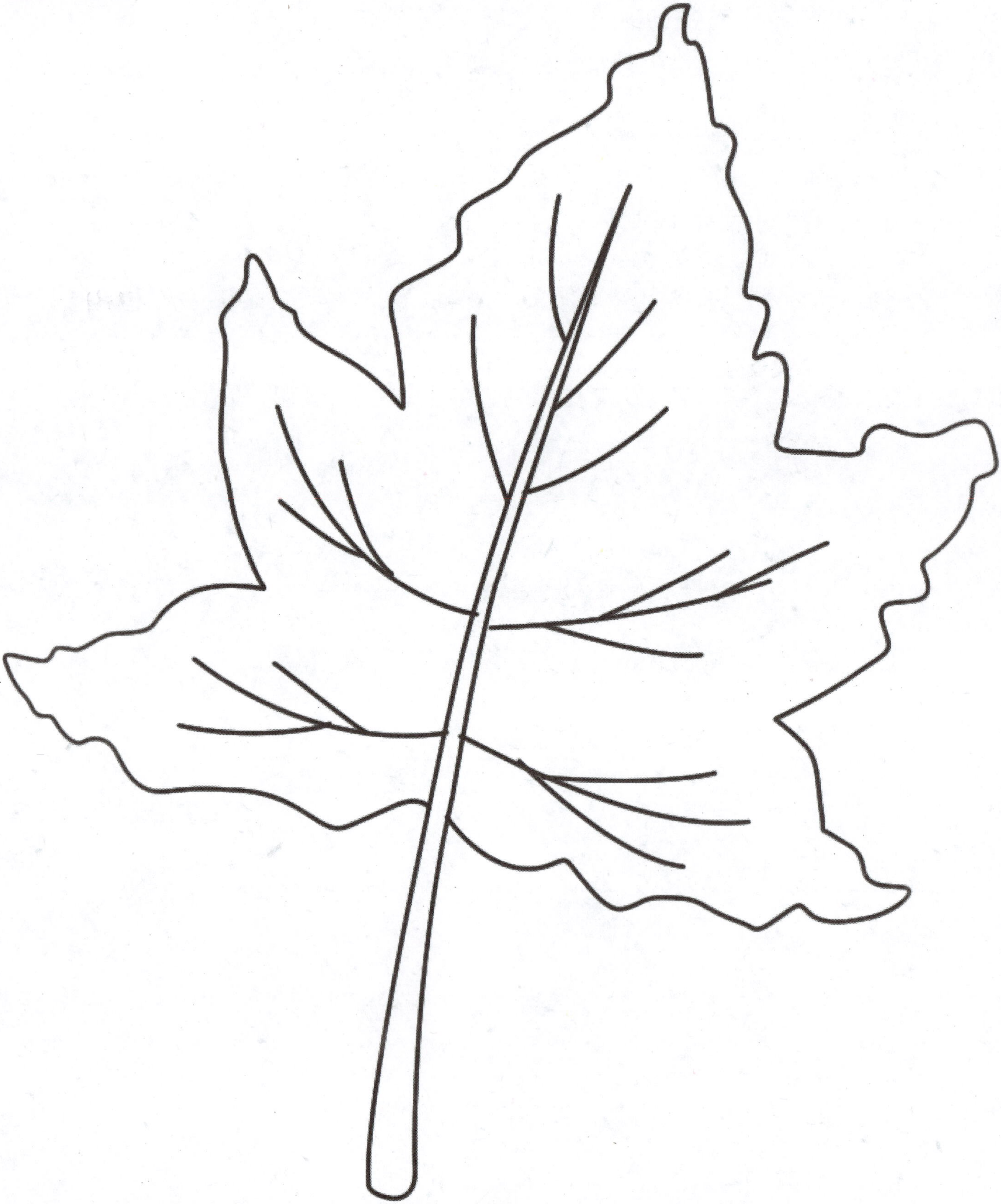

77 Connect the dots to complete the picture and colour it.

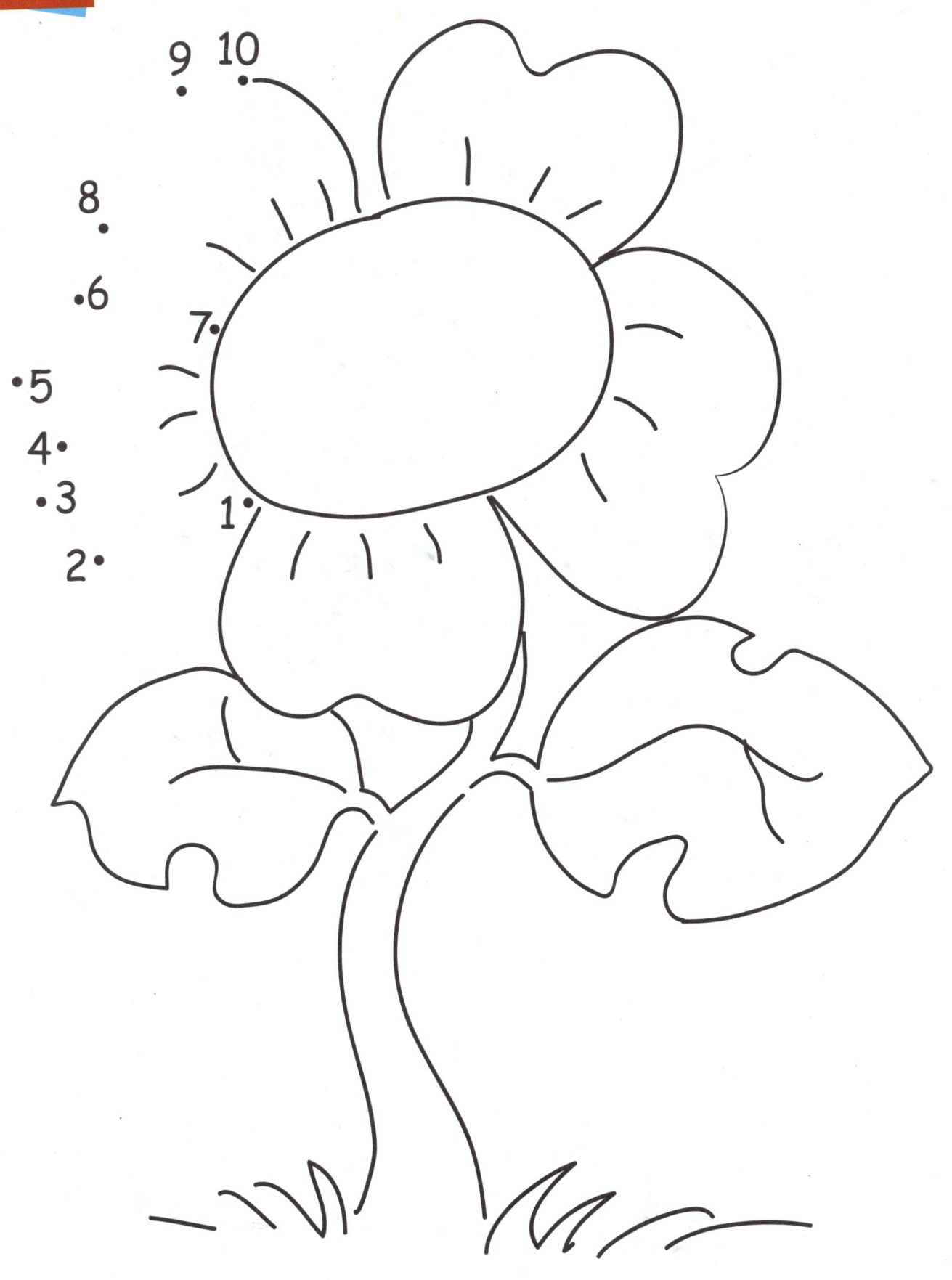

78 Find out the differences between the two pictures.

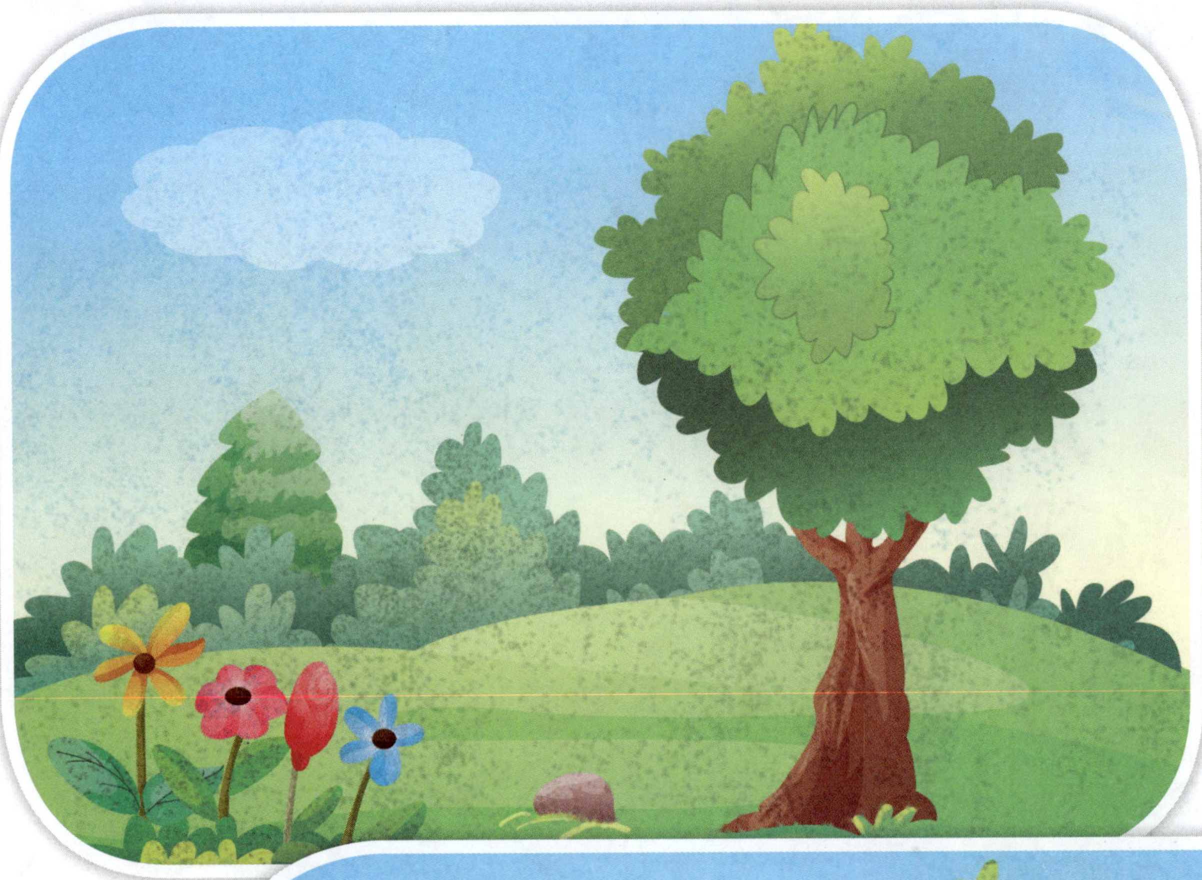

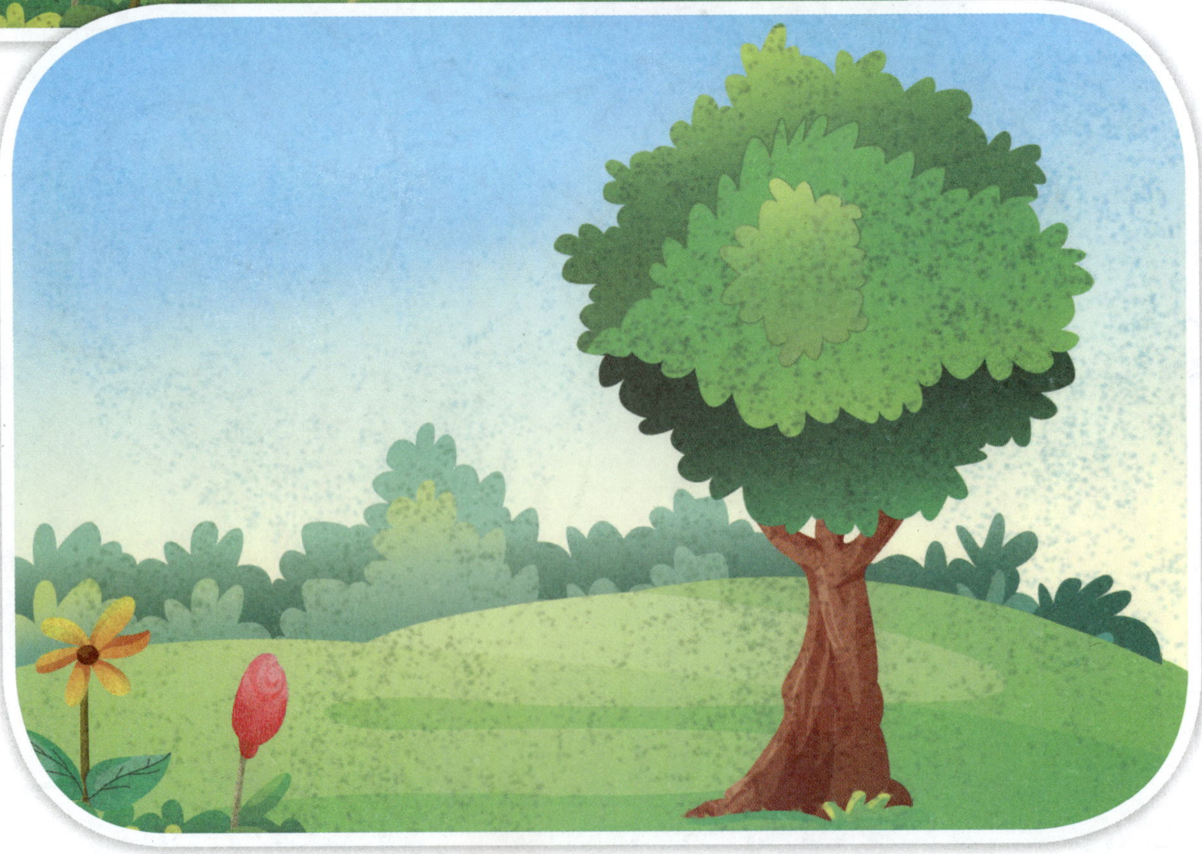

79 Help the boy reach the other end to plant a tree.

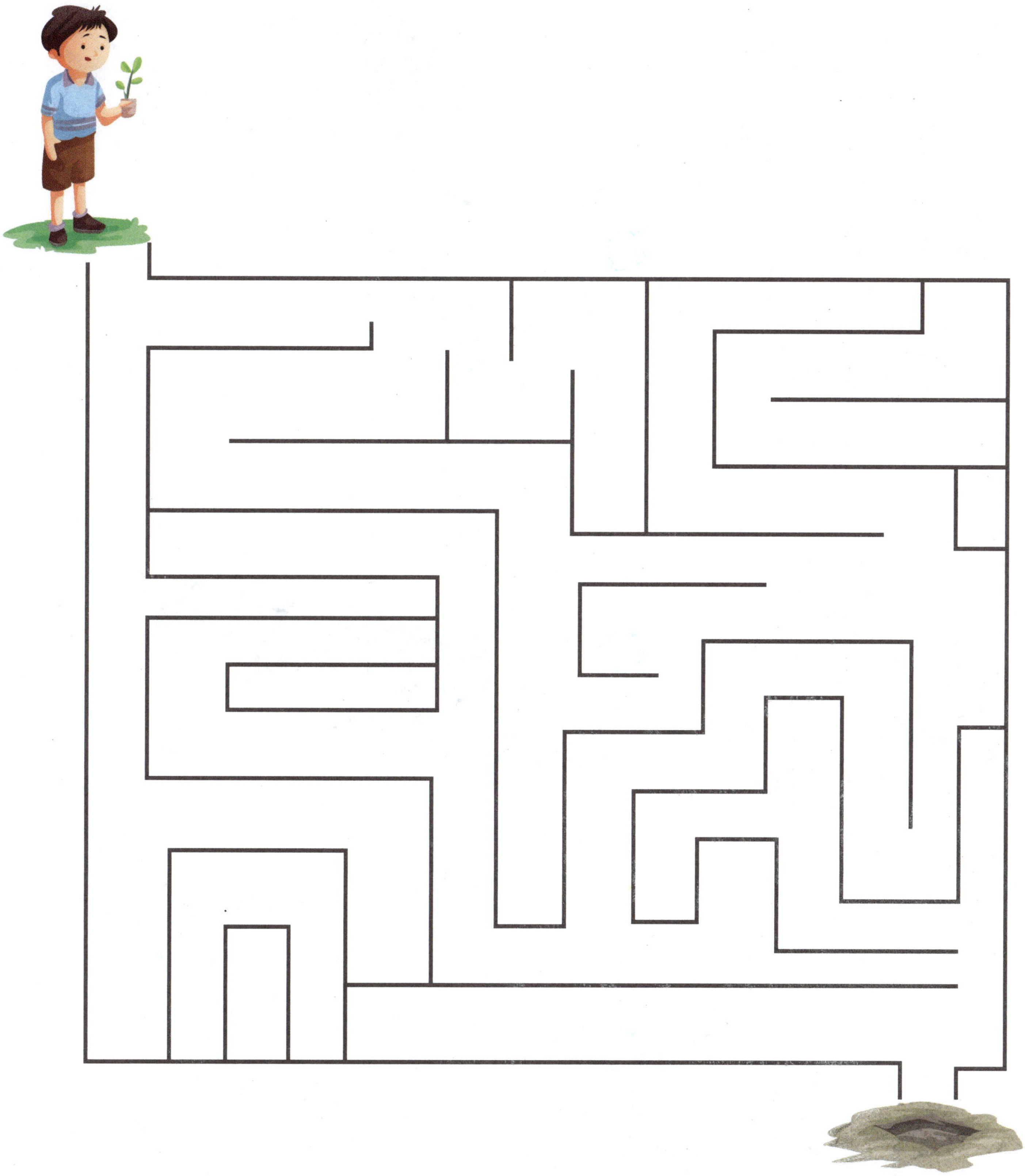

80 Circle the vegetables that grow on creepers.

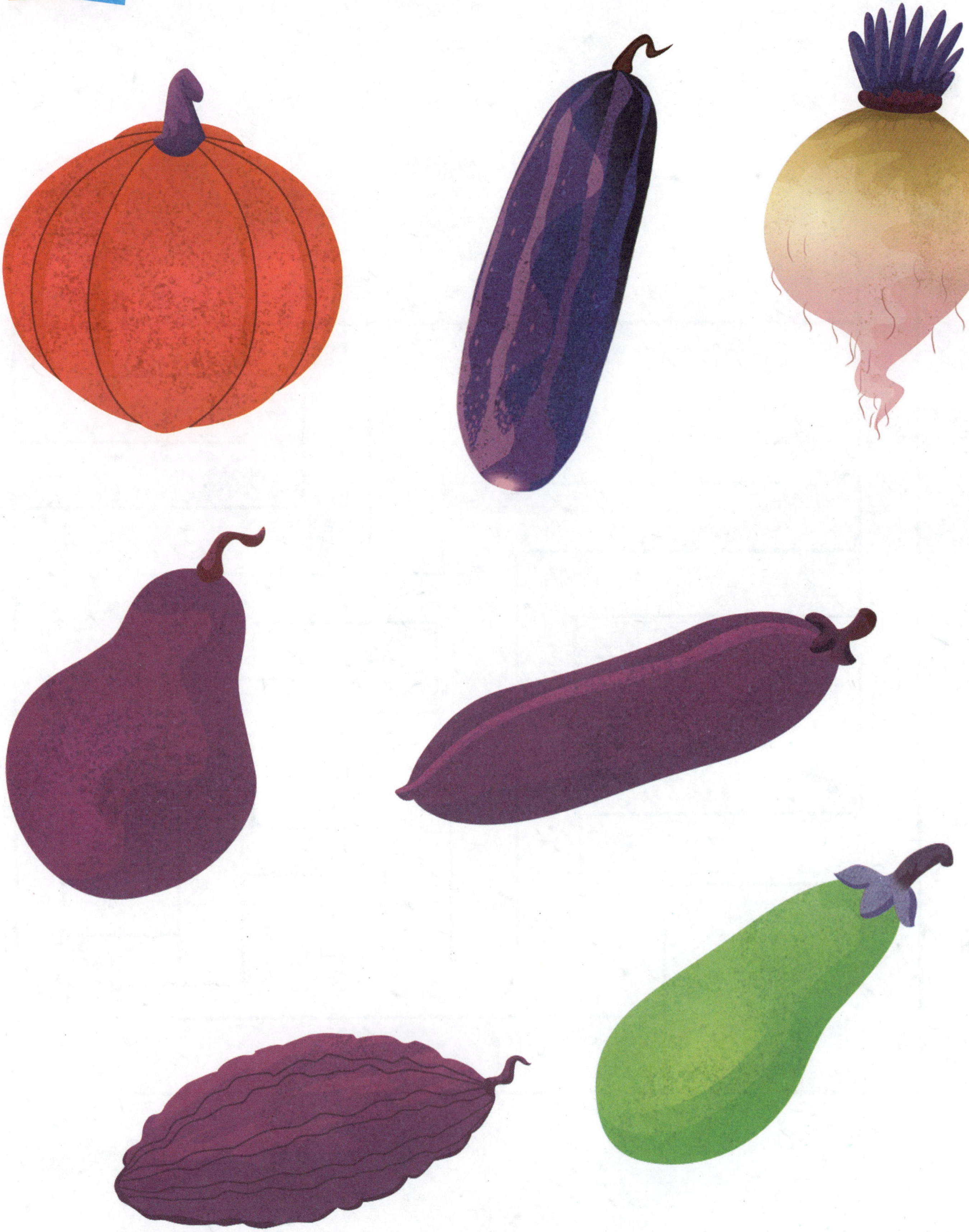

Draw a line from the picture of the herb to its name.

Oregano

Basil

Thyme

Dill

Sage

Parsley

Colour the tree.

83 Some plants have edible stems. Identify those plants in the pictures below and tick those.

POTATO

GINGER

SUGARCANE

LOTUS

CINNAMON

84 Plants, as you know, give us many things. Draw a line from the vegetable to its name.

Broccoli

Seeds

Carrot

Cabbage

85 Plants give us grains to eat. Identify the pictures and complete the name of the grain that the below plants produce.

R_c_ plant   W_ea_ plant   M_ze plant

Oil comes from plants. Fill in the blanks to complete the names of oil giving trees and plants.

CA_TOR

SUNFLO_ER

MUS_ARD

COC_NUT

OLI_E

Look at the puzzle and see if you can find out the words given in the text box.

Almond | Cedar | Coriander | Corn | Fig | Grape | Grass | Leeks | Melon | Olive | Mustard | Pomegranate | Wheat | Lentils | Barley

A	L	M	O	N	D	Y	C	U	F	C	N
Q	E	W	E	G	R	T	O	H	I	M	W
C	E	D	A	R	K	U	R	G	G	L	H
O	K	F	H	A	Z	I	N	D	S	K	E
R	S	N	K	S	X	J	K	B	M	D	A
I	S	C	L	S	C	L	L	N	U	B	T
A	E	P	O	S	H	E	Q	M	S	A	R
N	T	M	E	L	O	N	W	K	T	R	W
D	Y	G	J	U	L	T	T	J	A	L	H
E	I	C	K	I	I	I	O	T	R	E	E
R	O	X	L	O	V	L	P	E	D	Y	K
Q	U	Z	E	P	E	S	S	G	H	C	B
A	P	O	M	E	G	R	A	N	A	T	E

 **88** Rewrite the jumbled words using the clue from the box given below.

| Wheat | Almond | Stem | Leaves | Coconut |
| Coriander | Stalk | Vein |

TUNOCOC _____

TEAHW _____

REDNAIROC _____

DNOMLA _____

METS _____

SEVAEL _____

KLATS _____

NIEV _____

 Draw the grapes attaching it with the leaves and colour them.

 There are some plants whose bulbs are treated as food. Write their names below the pictures.

Garlic

Onion

 Plants produce seeds that form a major part of our food. Circle the plants that produce seeds.

 Choose right words from the box given below.

Sunlight | Water | Seeds | Seedling | Leafy | Food | Veins | Stem

Plants need ___ and ___ to make food.

We eat ___ of asparagus.

Plants grow from ____.

Cabbage is a _____ plant.

In a leaf, there are fine lines called _____.

Seeds from plants are used as _____.

Seed first develop into _____.

 Help the monkey reach the banana tree.

Identify the pictures below and write their names.

Join the dots to complete the picture and colour it.

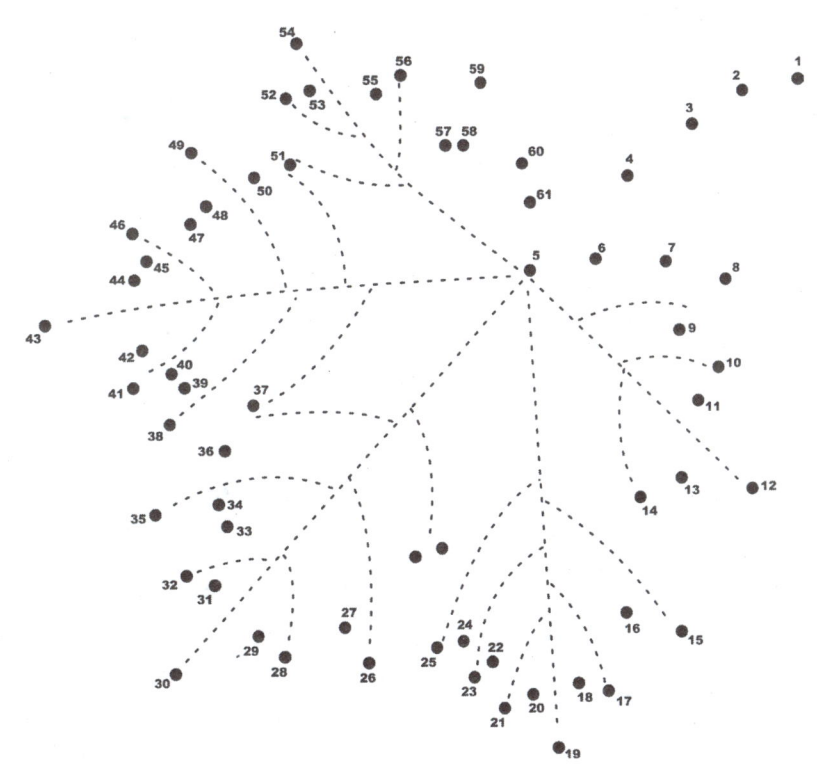

96 Complete the flower plant by pasting flower petals on it.

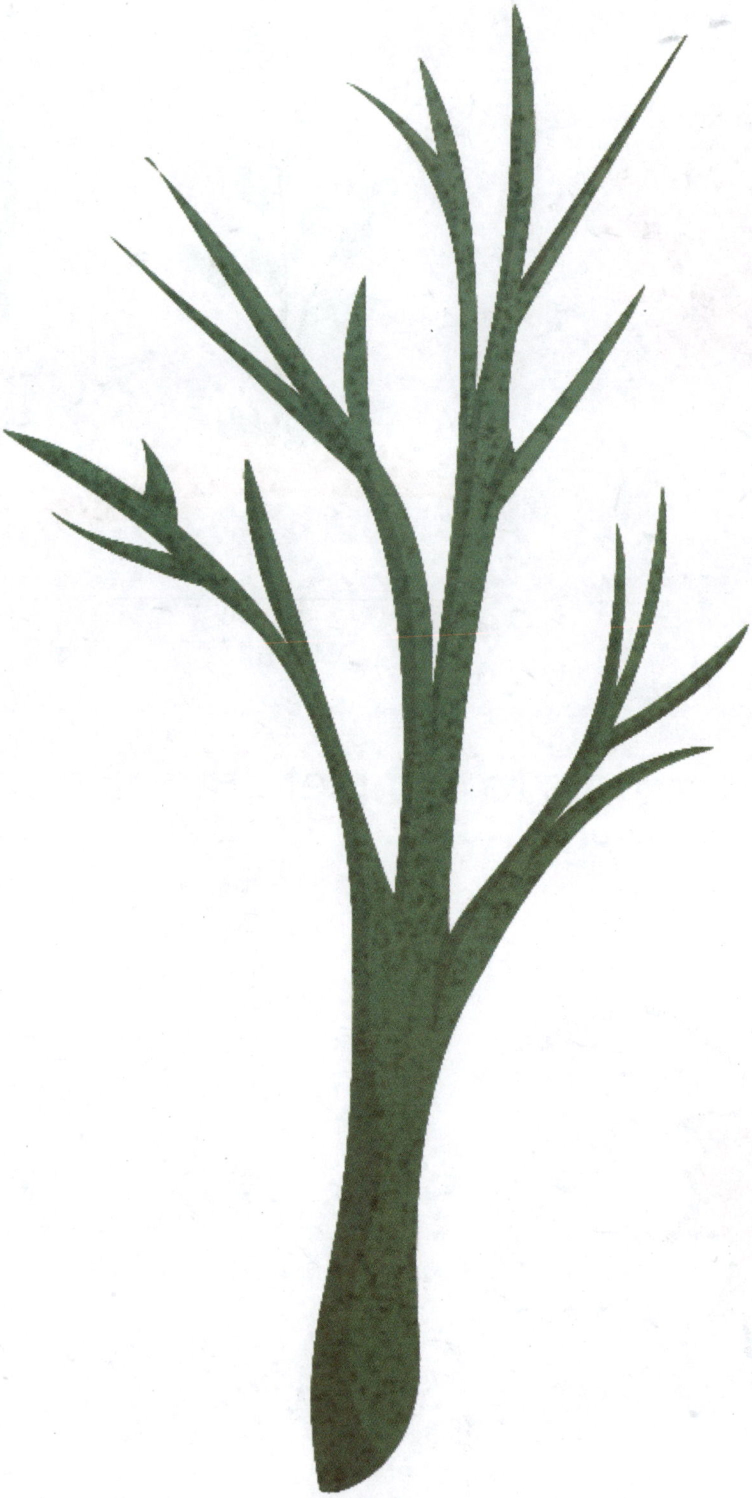

97 Fill the tree with leaves of your choice.

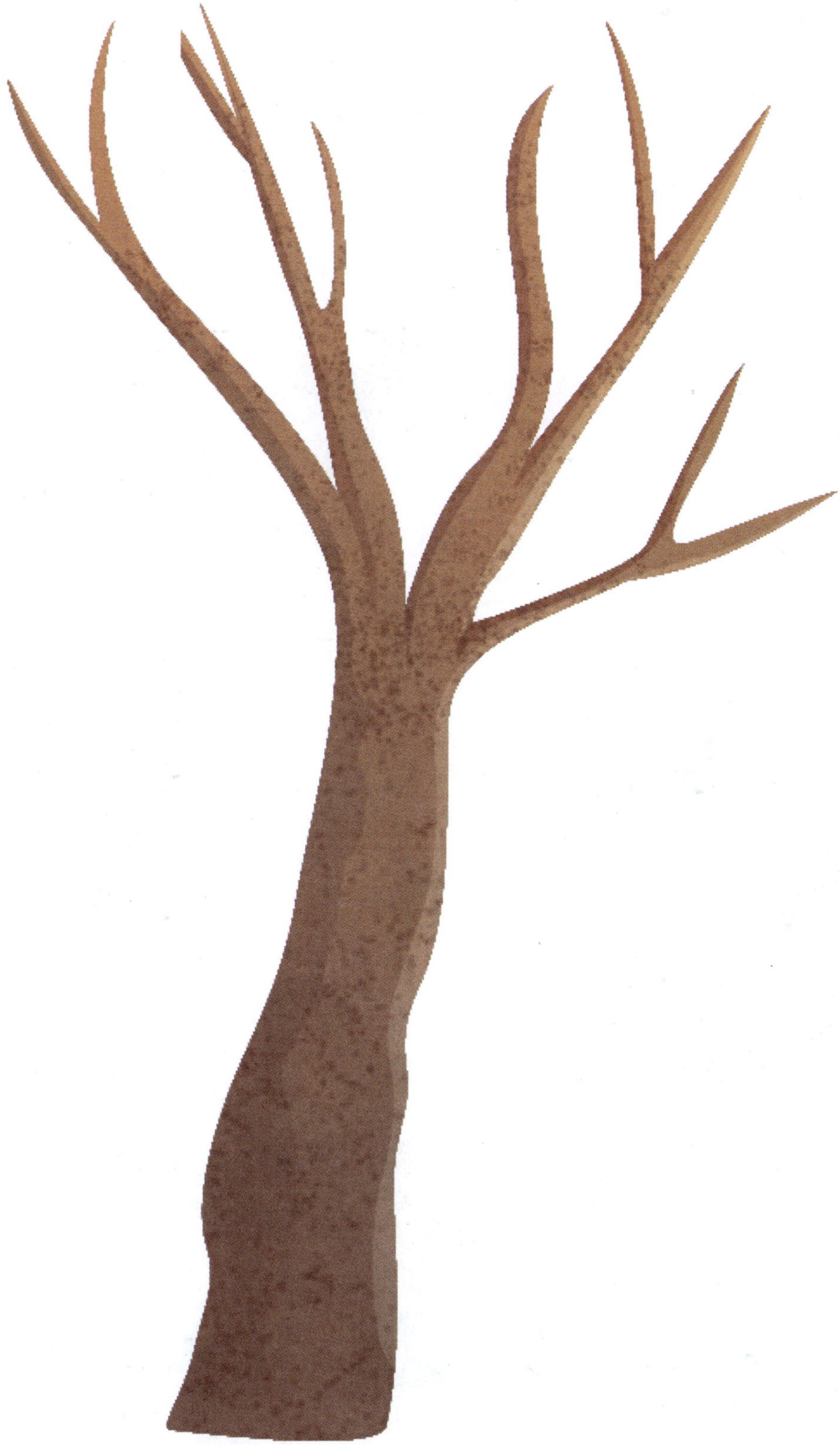

98 Fast blowing wind transfers the seeds of a flower from one place to another place. The seeds have been planted there. What will happen at the place after some days where the seeds have fallen?

 Unscramble the below words.

> Vein | Sugar | Garden | Trunk | Flower bed | Sapling | Conifer | Oregano

NIEV _____   GNILPAS _____

RAGUS _____   REFINOC _____

NEDRAG _____   ONAGERO _____

KNURT _____

DEB REWOLF _____

Complete the names of the below trees.

CED_R

BAL_AM FIR

AUS_RIAN PINE

SC_TS PINE

DOU_LAS FIR

BLUE SP_UCE